MIDNIGHT LULLABY

BOOKS BY JAMES D.F. HANNAH

The Henry Malone novels
Midnight Lullaby
Complicated Shadows
She Talks To Angels
Friend of the Devil
Behind the Wall of Sleep

The Parker County novels
The Righteous Path

JAMES D.F. HANNAH

MIDNIGHT LULLABY

A Henry Malone Novel

DOWN&OUT
BOOKS

Down & Out Books
3959 Van Dyke Road, Suite 265
Lutz, FL 33558
DownAndOutBooks.com

The characters and events in this book are fictitious. Any similarity to real persons, living or dead, is coincidental and not intended by the author.

Cover design by Eric Beetner

ISBN: 1-64396-171-3
ISBN-13: 978-1-64396-171-2

To the progeny. Without them, there's no story to tell.

CHAPTER 1

Christmas was coming. The plastic holly and fake trees had been side-by-side with the Halloween decorations since September, and Brenda Lee had been rockin' around the Christmas tree so long store cashiers were on suicide watch. By now the holiday loomed at every corner, like a schoolyard bully demanding your lunch money. Everything on TV had Christmas trees and styrofoam snow and lessons about the power of love, followed by ads for a Tom Cruise flick where he ran places and blew shit up.

I'd gone to Walmart to buy the groceries I'd throw away next week once they went bad. My knee let me get as far as the cereal aisle before the pain kicked in. I thought I could make it, at least until I couldn't, and I abandoned my cart in the coffee aisle, grabbing bread, milk, and half-and-half and leaving the rest. I gritted my teeth through the check-out and pushed back tears once I got to my car.

Pain burned like splinters of phosphorous through my knee. I lugged around twenty pounds more than my six-foot-one frame could handle, and my tendency toward gravy-heavy breakfasts at Tudor's didn't help.

I sat in the parking lot for a long time, hoping shit would stop hurting, knowing it wouldn't, and finally conceded defeat, swallowing a handful of painkillers from my supply in the glove compartment, washing it down with the milk and driving home.

A radio station had gone to an all-Christmas playlist, and

thirty percent of it was the Dan Fogelberg song about him meeting an ex at the grocery store. They were day-drinking a six-pack in their car as I pulled my Aztek into my driveway. I didn't recognize the Ford F-350 already there.

The guy on the front porch was fortyish, heavy around the middle, wearing a "Coal Keeps the Lights On" baseball cap and a Carhartt coat. He scratched at a graying Fu Manchu mustache. His skin had the permanent discoloration it gets after a decade of pulling coal, and the black dust shoves so deep into your pores there's no getting it out.

"You Henry Malone?" he said as I mounted the short set of stairs onto the porch.

"I am," I said.

He extended a hand. I took it. "I'm Mitch Fisher. How you doing?"

"I'm grand," I said. When he realized I didn't intend to shake his hand, it drew it back and shoved it back into his jacket pocket. "You didn't hear a dog bark on the porch, did you?"

"No. Why?"

"No reason," I said as I unlocked the front door and walked in, flipping on the lights behind me. Mitch Fisher followed right behind. "Yeah, go ahead and let yourself on in."

In the living room, one hundred twenty pounds of Bullmastiff stretched out across the couch, snoring as "Armageddon" flickered on the forty-three-inch flat-screen. If the end of the world wouldn't rouse Izzy, no reason to expect a truck in the driveway would do the job either.

"Hell of a watchdog," I said in her direction. An ear twitched, and she pushed her face into the cushions.

I made my way to the kitchen and put away the groceries. Fisher stood at the kitchen doorway, watching me like an admonished child at a parent.

"You're limping," he said.

"I am. My knee hurts."

"I mean, you're limping pretty bad."

"It hurts pretty bad."

"You might ought to get that looked at."

"Thanks, I hadn't thought of that. I'll jump right on it." I peered into the refrigerator. "You want something to drink? I got beer, milk, and half-and-half, if that's your thing."

"I'll take a beer if you've got one," he said.

I wanted to point out I'd specifically mentioned the beer, which more than implied I indeed had beer, but instead I handed him a bottle of Bud Light and took a diet Coke out for myself. He twisted the lid off of his bottle and took a long drink, then said, "You not having one?"

I shook my head. "Don't drink. Just keep 'em for company. On account I'm such a social creature."

That seemed an agreeable answer for him, which worked because I didn't plan on coming up with another one. I took my coat off, draped it on the back of a chair and took a seat. I motioned to the empty chair. "Help yourself."

He kept his coat on and sat down. He was younger than I'd thought, but life had packed years on him. He kept the beer bottle tight in thick, calloused hands.

"What can I do for you, Mitch Fisher?" I said.

"Jackie Hall told me I should come by, see you," he said.

"He say anything about calling first, and not just showing up unannounced on someone's doorstep?" I said. "What if I'd been out carousing or running around bare-assed naked?"

Fisher laughed. "Lt. Hall said you were a funny guy."

"Yeah, I'm hilarious. I suspect you're not here for the jokes, though."

He took another drink. "My sister's Bobbi Fisher."

"Your parents must be real proud, but that doesn't answer the question of what you want."

He cocked an eyebrow. "Don't you know who my sister is? Don't you watch the news?"

"I limit my news intake to anything about the royal family and if the Browns make it to the Super Bowl. Your sister marry a prince or get drafted as a running back?"

Fisher reached into his coat pocket and produced a newspaper clipping. He unfolded it on the table, smoothing it out before sliding it across to me.

Investigation Into Missing Mother
Stretches Into Second Month
By Jason O'Brien
Parker County Herald-Tribune

Authorities say that while there are no fresh leads into the disappearance of Parker County resident Bobbi Fisher, they are continuing to pursue the case while the mystery of what happened to the mother of two stretches into its second month.

State Police Lt. Jackson Hall said the toll-free telephone number started to accept tips into Fisher's disappearance is still receiving calls but has produced no new leads.

"This doesn't mean that people should stop calling," Hall said. "All this means is that we are now going back and reviewing previous leads and working to see where that goes. We are encouraging anyone with any information into Bobbi Fisher's disappearance to call. We want to return Ms. Fisher to her family."

Fisher, 27, of Serenity, was last seen Oct. 2 as she dropped her daughters off to daycare at 8 a.m. Police were called when she failed to report to work that day at McGinley and Kurt, the Serenity-based law firm where she worked as a secretary, and never came to pick her daughters up from day care.

Police found Fisher's car, a blue 2005 Ford Focus, abandoned off Rt. 232 the next day. A forensic investigation of the vehicle produced no results.

The picture of Bobbi Fisher showed a woman attractive if a little worn, the result of too much drugstore beauty product and too many late nights of beer and Marlboros. She was blonde with roots to make Alex Haley proud, a round, moon-shaped face, and almond-colored eyes. She wasn't my type, but she still would have been attractive even before last call.

I handed the clipping back to Fisher. "I'm sorry your sister's missing, but that's got nothing to do with me."

Fisher refolded the clipping and slipped it back into his coat. "You used to be a cop."

"'Used to be.' Past tense."

"Right, but he said you were good, and he thought you might help. You could look at things, see something that no one else is seeing."

A smile flickered across my face. "Lt. Hall told you that, huh?"

"Yes, sir."

I rested my forearms on the table. "Mr. Fisher, I think Lt. Hall might have overstated a few things. Whereas I used to be a state trooper, what I am now is an ex-cop on retirement disability. That limp you pointed out, it makes my life miserable most days, and it doesn't make me the best choice to play Jim Rockford. Besides that, I don't have any licensing or legal standing to be a private investigator."

Fisher took off his hat and ran his hand over his head, brushing down his thinning hair. "I didn't like coming here and asking you, but this was Lt. Hall's idea, Mr. Malone. Bobbi's a good mom, she loves her girls, and she wouldn't never just leave them, no word or nothing. The day care, the day it happened, called up me and my wife—my wife, her name's Jessie—and we picked the girls up and drove over to Bobbi's house and we waited with 'em and she never showed up. We called her cell phone over and over, and all it did was send to her voice mail. She just up and vanished."

Mitch Fisher's voice ached of concern, of worry, of fear, of loss—even if there was no actual knowledge of known loss yet. But it made me think about his nieces, and what it was like to find out your mother wasn't coming home.

I pushed myself out of the chair and opened up the junk

drawer, found a mechanical pencil and a notepad, and sat back down at the table. "Your sister, she got anyone who doesn't like her? An ex, or her boyfriend's got an ex?"

"Nah," he said. "She spent her time with her girls."

"How old are your nieces?" I said.

"The little one, she's four. Her name's Amelia. The older one, Becky, she's nine," he said. He finished his beer and set the empty bottle down.

"Want another?" I said. He said yes, and I got it for him. The painkillers were wearing off already, and I felt the blood coursing through my knee. I sucked air through my teeth and told myself I could take it. Mitch Fisher sipped his beer and was kind enough to not comment on me grimacing.

"How long were you a state trooper?" he said.

"Sixteen years," I said.

"What happened that you're not one anymore?"

"Shit that's neither here nor there. I'm sure you've been told this already, but there are certain realities you need to deal with, Mr. Fisher," I said.

"You're gonna tell me you don't know if you can find Bobbi," he said.

"I am. I'll bet Lt. Hall has said that by this point, finding your sister, the odds aren't good."

Fisher looked down at his beer bottle. "He's gone over it with us."

"If he's saying to not get your hopes up, then he's being honest with you, which you need to hear," I said. "I might not be able to find your sister, and even if I can, you may not like what I have to tell you. I can run down what the cops had, see if anything new comes up, but time's the disadvantage here. I'm one guy, and trails like this, they get cold quick."

Fisher scratched at the label on the beer bottle with his thumbnail. "You got kids?"

"I don't."

Fisher cast his eyes downward. His voice dropped low. "My

wife, she can't have babies," he said. "We tried, and nothing worked, so Bobbi's girls, my wife put all that love into them she couldn't put into ones of our own. But we ain't their parents, and Jessie's not their mom. They need their mother, and my wife needs to not raise those girls knowing they're not hers to have."

I nodded. "I'll check around, see what I find out," I said. "No promises. I can ask questions and make phone calls. Can't promise much past that."

He extended his hand toward me. "I appreciate you doing this, Mr. Malone."

I shook his hand. "It's Henry."

I locked the door behind him as he left and watched out the window as he drove away and the taillights faded into the darkness.

Back in the kitchen, I looked at the refrigerator's contents longer than I should have. There was fresh bread and milk, questionable eggs, cheese that wasn't improving with age, something that had once been a half-pound of hamburger, and four six-packs of Bud Light.

I closed the refrigerator door and opened a can of beef jerky on the counter next to it. Four truck tire-sized paws hit the living room floor, and Izzy lumbered in toward me. Even for food, that dog didn't get herself in a hurry.

I stood with arms crossed and tried to keep the jerky out of sight. She stopped and sat down in front of me and cocked her head to one side.

"Yes?" I said.

Izzy twisted her head to the other side, staring at me with brown eyes the size of coffee saucers. Drool gathered at her jowls.

I reached the jerky out toward her. She leaned forward and took it from my hand and laid on the floor to eat it. I patted her on the head and started a pot of coffee. It was late, but that didn't matter; I wasn't likely to be asleep for a while, anyway.

CHAPTER 2

I knew Jackie Hall from when we were both in uniform, stationed close to Morgantown. Back then, we'd both been tall and fit, in crisp-looking uniforms and high-and-tight haircuts, and there was no shortage of hot young things who appreciated a date who came ready with his own set of handcuffs. Jackie called them "badge bunnies."

He used to tell me stories about his uncle in New Jersey, around Paramus, pushing fifty back in the day but kept this rotating cycle of big-haired blondes with a thing for cops. Some of these girls, Jackie said, were young enough to be his uncle's daughter, as if his uncle would ever get married. To listen to Jackie, you'd have thought his uncle was a rock star.

Jackie and I were stationed together awhile out of the academy. Jackie was more motivated than I was, though, and he kept moving up the promotion ladder, while I preferred working the highways and responding to calls. He got himself a detective shield, a plain-clothed gig, and a transfer elsewhere, and I kept a cruiser and wrote tickets and as time wore on, I found someone steady to use my handcuffs with.

After the shooting and my life collapsing, I came back to Parker County. I didn't hear from Jackie. That was fine because I had gotten accustomed to feeling like a warning to others. Then last year I got Jackie's Christmas letter. It was one of those newsie things that talked about the toddler learning to walk and the summer vacation to Myrtle Beach.

There was a photo from the little studio in front of Walmart, of Jackie, a chunky brunette, and a two-year-old, all of them wearing identical sweaters with reindeer and snowmen on them. Jackie had put on a good fifty pounds, though it may have been closer to seventy-five. He looked like a goddamn fool. He also looked rather goddamn happy.

The return address was for Barlow, an unincorporated community there in Parker County. I called up the nearest state police outpost and got the bastard on the phone and found out he'd moved his way up to lieutenant and had been planted in Parker County a year earlier, a transfer request because his wife Livvie had family this way and she wanted to be closer to them on account of the baby.

We met that night, and I had a Coke and Jackie had a beer and he told me he hadn't planned on marriage, but this girl, she was an elementary school teacher and she had been the first one to wear down his reluctance.

"Besides," he'd said as he patted his gut, "I wasn't getting skinnier or better looking."

I told him I supposed not everyone could be his uncle. He laughed. "We should all be so fucking lucky."

The station was an old, flat building with a half-dozen state cruisers flanked in the parking lot. Painted on the top glass half of his office door was "Jackson Hall, Lieutenant, West Virginia State Police." Jackie was behind his desk in an armless chair with two inches of him spilling out over each side, taking a bite of a foot-long meatball sub as I walked in.

He jerked forward as the door opened and a dollop of marinara dripped from the end of the sandwich onto his tie. He slapped the sandwich down on his desk and reached for a napkin.

"Goddammit, Henry, you can't just let a man eat in peace?"

He wiped at his tie, smearing sauce.

I sat down in the visitor's chair. "I doubt anyone's gonna start a canned food drive so you don't waste away to nothing."

Jackie tossed the napkin into the trash can next to his desk. "I know you didn't come here just to be an asshole, since you can be an asshole anywhere. I'm guessing you talked to Mitch Fisher?"

"I did."

"You gonna do it?"

"You think I have anything to contribute that your guys haven't already?"

He sucked up soda from a takeaway cup. "Man wants answers, and you can't fault him for that. Him and his wife, those little girls, there's gotta be something we can tell them at some point."

"You can tell them the goddamn truth, which is that she's probably dead somewhere, and they can find those girls a good therapist and let 'em spend the rest of their lives working their shit out. Happens all the time. News is filled with it, folks vanishing and never get found. It's the reason Nancy Grace wakes up every fuckin' morning."

"That they do, and there's almost always someone somewhere wondering what the fuck happened to them. No one wants to grow up not knowing if their mother's dead or alive. You know this better than anyone, Henry."

For a second, I debated coming out of the chair and using his sauce-stained tie to choke the fat asshole until his vision went black and he could answer the secrets of the universe. Most people who knew about my mother had the common decency to not play on that. Not Jackie, though.

I opted to let him live, however, and instead I took out my pencil and notepad. "Tell me about Bobbi Fisher."

"Not much to tell. Two kids. Works at that law place in town with the jingle in the TV ads."

"McGinley and Kurt."

Jackie winked and shot me with his forefinger and thumb. "That's the one."

"Don't do that," I said. "You look like a douche. What about an ex-husband? Boyfriend?"

"No husband. Kids' daddy went for a drive and never looked back. No boyfriend that anyone knows about."

"She owe anyone money? Get along with her family? Was she into drugs?"

He counted each off on his fingers. "No, yes, and no. Henry, do you not think any of this is stuff we didn't ask already?"

"Well, fuck me running, Jackie. I just walked into this mess, and since reading minds isn't in my skill set, I might end up asking a question that's already been asked."

Jackie opened a desk drawer and handed me a manila folder. "You been keeping up with any of this?" he said.

"Nope. Why should I?"

"Because it's all over every goddamn news broadcast and on the front page of the newspaper every day."

"I let my paper subscription lapse. They print the comics too small, and 'Peanuts' is nothing but reruns, anyway."

The file Jackie gave me was thin, consisting of the initial missing person report, transcripts of interviews, follow-up reports, and photographs of Bobbi Fisher. The photos were of her and her daughters at a Chuck E. Cheese, others with a group of women I guessed were co-workers, and another from what I presumed to be a family picnic, where I recognized Mitch Fisher.

"What you're telling me," I said, "is that you've got nothing, and from this pile of sow's ears you want me to shit a silk purse."

Jackie folded his hands together and rested his palms on the back on his head. It was chilly outside, it wasn't much better inside, and Jackie still had geometrically perfect sweat circles underneath each arm. "You might be right, that you'd be better off sitting on your ass with your goddamn gimpy leg."

I glanced up. "Antiperspirant, Jackie. Check into it."

Jackie shot looks at his armpits and dropped his arms down onto his desk. His face flushed red. "Sweating is a sign of a healthy system."

"Then you're Olympic-level, brother," I said. "And besides, someone has to show you assholes how to do some police work. It's obvious you don't have a clue what the hell you're doing."

"We all can't be beautiful and brilliant like you, Henry." Jackie leaned back in his chair and the springs groaned in misery.

I snapped a picture frame off the desk. Jackie and the family. "Family's looking fat and happy."

"Mostly fat," he said. "Wife likes to make gravy, and she's good at it." He huffed a breath. "You ever talk to Maggie?"

I handed him back the case folder. "Sometimes. She calls, or I call her."

Jackie nodded. I could tell he wasn't sure what to say. I wasn't sure myself.

He leaned forward, folded his hands together on the desk. "The Fisher family doesn't have the money it'd take to get answers in this," he said. "I thought you could at least show them there may never be an answer."

"Plenty of people go through life without answers, Jackie. But why don't you tell me what you think happened."

Jackie drank more soda. "There's two options. First, that she shows up somewhere down south in a few months, working as a waitress at a truck stop, a stripper, some bullshit like that, because she had enough and snapped and couldn't handle it anymore, whatever 'it' was. Or the second, which is more likely, is that in four or five years, someone'll be clearing out a slab of mountainside, and there'll be a bunch of bones that turn up, and that's what's gonna be left of Bobbi Fisher. We'll kind of have an answer at that point, since it's not likely she drifted off into the hills and threw herself in a hole. But when that happens, it still won't answer questions; they'll just have something to bury. Which I suppose was buried already, so irony." He threw his hands into the air. "That's just me, though, being a prick of a cop. Big, fat, cynical bastard."

"You said she wasn't into anything suspicious."

"That's just what people told us. And what's the first thing

we both know about people?"
    "That they lie like motherfuckers,"
    "Exactly," he said.

CHAPTER 3

It's not that I hate attorneys; it's just my experience with them is that they're scum-sucking bottom feeders who'd whore their mothers out for a quarter. A place like McGinley and Kurt would probably offer a stamped customer card for the experience.

McGinley and Kurt was a franchised firm with offices in store fronts across the state, specializing in Social Security and medical malpractice cases. You passed their billboards up and down the interstate, imploring you to call so they could sue someone for you. Their commercials ran during the local news and were notorious for production values that would shame porn. But they had a jingle, and it was only slightly less catchy than cholera:

We're there for you, we're by your side
You're not alone, we're along for the ride;
So if you get injured, if you've been hurt
Just pick up the phone and call McGinley and Kurt.

It made you want to die every time you heard it.

The primary offices were in a Civil War-era two-story with Greek pillars and a balcony. Wilson McGinley's office was at the end of the second-story hallway, just off a spiral staircase I expected Scarlett O'Hara to descend from. McGinley sat on the opposite side of a desk a fraction smaller than a hockey rink.

I wore a sports coat from the back of my closet, thrown on over a blue button-down from Goodwill and the best blue jeans I owned. There hadn't been time to run by the barber college to get a haircut; McGinley had agreed to meet me that day after I'd called to set up an appointment. I kept brushing back the hair that hung over the tops of my ears.

McGinley smiled as he ran chunky fingers across the polished surface of the desk. He was late-in-life comfortable, thick in the middle, wearing a suit that hadn't been in style when he'd bought it at Sears twenty years prior. McGinley was the official commercial spokesman for the firm, the smiling face that appeared in thirty-second intervals across the area. He needed to stop coloring his hair with cheap product; it gave his hair a purple tint to it that made him seem alien.

"I can't say I'm familiar with your name, Mr. Malone," he said. "We work with most investigative firms in this area, and throughout the state, and your name isn't one that—"

"I'm not with an agency," I said.

He arched his eyebrows. It took a lot of work, but he finally got the flesh around his forehead to move. "Oh, so you're free-lance?"

"Not really. I'm looking into Ms. Fisher's disappearance as a favor for her brother."

"I see," he said, resting his hands on his gut. "Then you have a background in this sort of thing, I would presume."

I chewed on the inside of my cheek. "I was a state police trooper."

"Ah. Well, to be honest, I'm not sure there's much that we can answer now we couldn't answer…it's been what, a month now?"

"More than two months."

McGinley sat back in his chair. Little shit-eating smile on his face. Preparing to pass on some learned knowledge and shit. Man, but I wanted to punch the old coot.

"Mr. Malone, it's my experience that, for many women who come to work here, life is very—" He lifted his head and looked skyward. "Transitory, I suppose, is the right word. Not to sound harsh, but for many of our female employees, they're only here until they find something that seems like a better offer, and when they leave, they don't always offer the courtesy of giving goodbyes."

"Bobbi Fisher has two daughters. She doesn't seem the type who would up and walk away from that."

McKinley laughed. It wasn't a pleasant sound. "Your optimism is charming, Mr. Malone, and maybe I've spent too many years seeing the worst in people, but with what I know of the world, a woman will sell her children out in a heartbeat if she sees something with a big enough dick or a big enough wallet."

I leaned forward until I could rest my forearms on the desk surface, pushing back the wood-and-brass "Wilson McGinley" nameplate, the heavy antique desk lamp, the desk calendar with nothing written on it, even the pencil holder, scooting them all back and making sure they made a scratching sound. It cut fresh grooves into the desktop.

"I appreciate that, Mr. McGinley," I said with a smile, "but I'd still like to talk about Bobbi Fisher."

McGinley stared at me like I had just ripped the rankest fart imaginable, something born of ramps and pinto beans. "This desk is two hundred years old, and I've spent a sizable amount of money restoring it, and you are ruining it."

I smiled like the village idiot. "Oops," I said. "Excuse the hell out of me." I settled back into my chair.

McGinley stretched across the desk and pushed everything back into place. He brushed imaginary crumbs off of the front of his suit and said, "Ms. Fisher's work was secretarial, and that was with different associates. I can't speak personally about her. I knew her if I saw her in the halls, said hi to her, but we weren't exchanging Christmas cards. The office cards, yes, but nothing personal."

I took my notebook and mechanical pencil out of my jacket. "Which attorneys worked with Bobbi?"

"I'll have you talk to Doria Newland," he said. "She's the head of administrative services, so she's the person who can tell you the most about Ms. Fisher."

I wrote the name down and slipped the notebook back into my jacket pocket. "If you didn't know Bobbi, why did you even agree to talk to me? Why not just refer me to this Doria Newland to start with?"

He bored holes through me with hooded eyes. "It was what they term 'professional courtesy,' which you would understand if you behaved like a professional, Mr. Malone." He pushed his chair away from his desk, rising to his feet.

"Funny; you look taller on TV," I said.

He flashed a smile that reeked of impatience and came around the desk. It was clear it was my time to go. He walked me to his office door, opened it, and motioned me out.

"I hope the best in finding Ms. Fisher," he said. He didn't offer to shake my hand, and the door closed in my face. I turned to look at his secretary, a gum-chewing Millennial playing "Candy Crush" on her computer.

"I did think he'd be taller," I said to her. She clicked her mouse and obliterated a line of jellybeans without looking at me.

CHAPTER 4

I expected Doria Newland to look like Ms. Hathaway from "The Beverly Hillbillies." That was the only point of reference I had for someone running a secretarial pool: a spinster bulldog in polyester with a stick not just shoved up her ass, but flipped sideways for emphasis.

Doria Newland was outside, sitting in one of the rocking chairs set across the wide back porch. The temperature was moderate, hanging in the forties, but with all the moisture sucked from the air, every breath you drew was as raw and dry as sand. You'd have mistaken it for October except for the yellowed paper Santa Clauses in the windows. That, and that goddamned Dan Fogelberg song.

Doria took a deep pull off of a Marlboro Light as I came around the corner of the building. She had dirty blonde hair streaked with gray and pulled into a loose ponytail, wearing an oversized cardigan and a T-shirt and dark skinny jeans that couldn't hide her curves. She glanced over at me and knocked a little ash off her cigarette and said, "Can I help you?"

"Only if you're Doria Newland," I said as I stepped up the porch stairs.

"You're in luck." She took a last draw off the cigarette, crushed it out on the porch floor and flicked it into the grass with her foot. "What can I do for you?"

Her expression never changed as I explained everything, just nodding and mumbling "mmm-hmmm." When I finished, she fished a pack of cigarettes from her purse and lit a fresh one.

"You plan on finding her?" she said as she blew smoke through pursed lips.

"I plan on looking for answers."

She smiled. Tiny lines formed around the corners of her eyes. "That's good. That's like what the assholes here tell you to say on the stand. Gives a response that satisfies the question without answering it. A commitment that makes you sound real non-committal."

"I'm new eyes, that's all," I said. "Mind if I have a seat?"

"I'm not likely to stop you."

I sat down in the rocking chair next to hers.

"So, Doria, what d'you think of Bobbi?" I said.

Doria exhaled smoke, stretching her neck out in the action. She had a long, thin throat, with tiny white streaks that hadn't gotten dark from the tanning bed.

"Bobbi's a nice enough kid," Doria said. "Had maybe a year of community college behind her when she got here. She was smart, though, and she worked hard." She paused for a moment. "'Smart' might be generous here."

"Why do you say that?"

She chewed on her bottom lip. It was a very nice bottom lip. "It wasn't that she was dumb. 'Naïve' is closer to the truth." She sighed. "I didn't say anything to the cops the first time around, because I hoped they might find her alive, but that doesn't seem to be a realistic expectation anymore."

I shrugged. "I'd think finding her regardless would be preferable to not finding her."

"I guess it would be. Anyway, Bobbi, she walked in here, had lots of enthusiasm, was a hard worker. All of that cliched bullshit people always give when they talk about someone like her, it was all true with her. She did the long hours, the working on weekends, never complaining, always smiling, and she always did it like a professional. I never once had an issue with her work ethic."

"I'm sensing that there's a 'but' coming with this."

"But—" She stretched the word out to multiple syllables and smiled. "—she was young, and single, and she said she'd been in some bad relationships, and I think she felt like a lot of these girls who are still looking for that white knight to come along and rescue them."

"Did someone here offer to ride up and save her?"

Doria put her hands on her calves and pushed herself up. "Sometimes, Mr. Malone, you know when you've already said too much before you've said much of anything. I believe I'm hitting that point. So if you'll excuse me, I've got work to get done."

I stepped in front of her as she turned toward the door. She bristled slightly, drawing her body back, coiling tense, as the door opened. A youngish guy, firm underneath his gray suit and holding a cigarette and lighter, looked at me. To Doria, he said, "Everything good here?"

She glanced at me. I took a step back.

To the guy, she said, "Yeah, everything's fine. Give us a few?"

The guy's expression said he was trying to figure out if he could kick my ass. The answer was probably yes.

Doria smiled at him. "It's good, Scott. I promise."

He shrugged and said, "Whatever. My lungs will be grateful for the reprieve." He tucked the cigarette and lighter into his jacket pocket and stepped back inside, closing the door behind him.

I took another step back, put more space between us. "I'm just trying to find two little girls' mother," I said. "I'm not gonna make your life difficult, but I will be super appreciative if you can tell me anything that might help me find Bobbi."

She chewed her lip more. It was a distracting habit, more for me than her. "Not here," she said. "Tonight. You know Marlowe's?"

I did. It was a dive joint stuck in the corner of an ancient strip mall, nothing left to the thing but a call center, a Laundromat, an everything-for-a-dollar store, and the bar.

"I'll be there about ten," she said. "See you there."

She moved past me, brushing her arm along mine and smiling before disappearing inside.

CHAPTER 5

Once I was home, Izzy needed to piss, so I walked out with her, watching her tear her way across the yard, stopping to sniff and squat and leave her mark and repeat the process enough times that I wondered how much urine one dog could contain. When said dog is the size of a bull moose, it's a lot.

We came inside as the mountains swallowed the last bits of sunlight and the sky turned black and starless. My cell phone rang as I set the kettle on the stove. The caller ID read Maggie's number. I sucked in a lungful of air before answering.

"Hey," I said. It was one of my smoother lines.

"Hey yourself, soldier," she said. Music played in the background. It sounded like The Eagles, which meant Duffy's, a place on High Street in Morgantown that Maggie liked. Drinkers took their drinking seriously at Duffy's, and "Greatest Hits, Volume One" was often the evening's soundtrack. I pictured everything about the moment. "Take It to the Limit" was muffled, which put her right outside the door, to the side, under the entrance awning. People made plenty of phone calls from that spot. Promises of "just one more" and they'll be home. Lots of lies told underneath that awning. My knowledge of the bar's geography maybe meant I had told my own lies there.

"How you doing?" I said.

"Great. Thinking about you. Wanted to call."

She wasn't drunk yet, but the wheels were pointed in that

22

direction. I recognized it in her voice, where her words were getting loose. She was about three beers in.

"I'm glad you called," I said. "What are you up to?"

"Nothing much. Our education reporter got a job doing state government PR down in Charleston. We're celebrating her leaving. We're so happy about it, we even invited her."

"Good for her."

"Fuck that shit. Snooty bitch won't last six months."

"Oh, well then, fuck her."

Maggie laughed. "Right. Exactly. Fuck her." She laughed again, harder. No one found Maggie as funny as she found herself. It was a trait I'd found endearing, whereas it pissed everyone else off. She cleared her throat. "So you know, I've got an interview for a gig in Philadelphia."

My stomach sank. "Newspaper?"

"Yeah. Working the city desk."

"You on the desk? What the hell happened? Have you had a head injury?"

"I'm being realistic, Henry. Time I stop acting like I'm gonna change the world or the Pulitzer committee is gonna call anytime soon. This is better money and steady hours."

"But Philadelphia is...so goddamn far," I said. "The other side of the state. What about Pittsburgh? Did you look there? Another paper in West Virginia?"

The connection got quiet.

"Hello? Maggie?" I said. "Maggie?"

"I'm here," she said, her voice soft. "I should go. They're wanting to move on to another bar—"

"Sure, but can we talk about this? That's a lot to process."

"It's a job. The interview's next week. I'll let you know what happens."

"Okay. Thanks. Have a good time tonight. Be safe."

"I will. I love you, Henry."

"I love you too, Mags."

The line fell silent.

The kettle whistled. I turned off the burner and opened the refrigerator and got a beer.

CHAPTER 6

Here's the thing about Alcoholics Anonymous meetings: never go BEFORE you plan to hit a bender. You'll end up washed over by the vibes of "one day at a time" and "easy does it" and "live in the now" and "we're all here because we're all not here" and next thing you know you're somewhere having coffee with a half-dozen other slobs as bad off as you, instead of getting the righteous buzz you so desired.

It's always better to find a meeting afterwards, while there's still a twinge of hangover and you'd rather be somewhere where they serve biscuits and gravy twenty-four hours a day, and instead there you are, listening to all the same shit you've heard at every other meeting, drinking the same shitty coffee, struggling to remember why all of this seemed like a good idea to begin with, but satisfied in the knowledge it's always better to beg forgiveness than it is to ask permission.

Thought processes like this explain why I'm a shitty sponsor.

Serenity is the county seat for Parker County, the third-largest county in West Virginia by sheer land mass, covering about a thousand square miles. If you believed the last census, there's thirty-eight thousand souls in the county's entirety, and just less than half of them are in Serenity. The rest are scattered throughout hollers and tiny unincorporated burgs that barely qualify as geographic blips. On maps, you'd mistake them as printing errors; "blink and you'll miss it" doesn't do them justice.

Coal grew the county for years, until accountants and actuaries figured out some seams weren't worth the money it took to clean them out. When the jobs left, so did most of the people, though the die-hards stayed, folks who owned land, farmed and raised animals and could still make something of their lives. Some stayed because they were out of options, so they became the third generation squeezing out an existence in run-down trailers or dilapidated houses, all within spitting distance of the rest of their relations.

Technology changes shifted how they mine coal, though, and when the seams became worth mining again, a lucky few, they got those jobs and clung to them until they left finger imprints. They slapped bumper stickers on their pickup trucks that read "If You Don't Support Coal, Just Sit In the Dark!" and kept right on like the past fifty years had never happened, not understanding they're the only ones who haven't realized the sun's coming up, and no party lasts forever.

St. Anthony's, the Catholic church, held meetings every night at eight, in a small room downstairs, set away from everything so the drunks wouldn't disturb evening Mass or baby showers or whatever else happens in a church when they aren't telling you how you're going to hell. There were other meetings scheduled throughout Parker County, but St. Anthony's was the most consistent, the one you knew you could turn to every night.

I recognized a lot of the faces. With small towns, you learn the faces and the stories and the glorious disasters that our lives tend to be. It doesn't provide much variety in the meetings, but becomes a comfort, the familiarity of knowing that there's someone out there with a story worse than yours, and you'll get to hear it if you show up and pay your dollar cover when they pass the basket around.

Woody chaired the meeting. Woody had been my sponsor since I'd left Morgantown and come back to Parker County, metaphorical hat in hand. He was a thin guy, built out of nothing but sharp right turns, with graying hair to his shoulders and a face craggy enough to make Sam Elliot look like a member of a boy band. I'd never seen him in anything but 501s and battered work boots and black T-shirts. Today was no different, though he was also wearing a red hoodie, a slight concession to winter weather.

Chairing a meeting meant keeping everyone on task, which is like herding cats when you're talking about alcoholics. This was open discussion, so everyone went around the room and talked about their drinking or the fact that they weren't drinking, and rah-rah sis boom fucking bah for them. The hour passed with minutes dragging along on their bellies until we stood and held hands and closed with the Lord's Prayer.

I always said the prayer, rote memorization after years spent in Baptist churches where threats of eternal damnation had hung over my head for every time I cranked off a shot into an used gym sock because I was fifteen and had nothing on my mind but boobs and an absolute dearth of offers from any girls to help relieve the pressure. I wasn't sure anymore I believed the words, but I said them anyway, the capstone to the hour. It didn't feel right otherwise, the meeting incomplete without the half-hearted recitation. I didn't think about what it meant, just using the familiarity to let me know I was done for the night.

The temperature had dropped, and it was colder than a well-digger's ass, but that never discouraged smokers after an AA meeting. It sure as hell didn't discourage me, and I bummed a cigarette from Woody.

"Haven't seen you in a while," he said. He'd grown a beard since I'd seen him a few weeks earlier. Woody was a guy, had a five o'clock shadow by noon. He might have grown it since breakfast.

"Been busy," I said.

"You haven't called, either."

"Part and parcel of that 'been busy' thing."

He nodded. "Drinking?"

I shook my head.

"You lying?"

"An alcoholic lie about drinking? How dare you."

Woody didn't smile so much as push up one corner of his mouth for a second, then let it go. I always wondered if this was an odd twerk of his, or if he'd had a stroke. I'd never asked, partially because it seemed rude, and mostly because I'd never given enough of a fuck to bother asking.

"How you doing?" he said.

"Like Sheila E. said, living the glamorous life."

He crushed his cigarette underneath his steel-toed boot and lit another. "Sounds like you're awesome."

"King of the world."

"Nice you've got time to hang out with us rabble."

I put out my cigarette. "Gotta get home. Plans tonight." I smiled. "With a lady."

"Sure thing," he said, not giving two good goddamns. "Wanna come out and shoot, next day or two?"

Woody owned sixty-five acres of farmland that now sat fallow and empty except for his old house, and the personal shooting range behind it. Despite that, on any given day he looked twenty bucks away from homelessness. Woody had cash somewhere. I'd never asked about it, either. I suppose my lack of questions asked pointed toward something about my cop abilities.

"Sounds good," I said. "I'll drop a dime in your direction."

"You do that," he said. "Be careful."

I was already walking away when he said it. I stopped and turned and started to say something witty, but he was already talking to someone else from the meeting. Just as well. I might need that clever retort another day.

CHAPTER 7

I was already there when Doria got to Marlowe's. I was at the bar, sipping a Michelob, telling myself I could have two but no more.

After it became clear I couldn't continue being the cop I wanted to be, and Maggie told me she needed space away from me, I dragged myself back to Serenity, and Parker County, because that's what you do when you lose everything, right? You go home.

The first year back was okay. I stayed sober, and I kept up with physical therapy. Then things went stagnant, and I blew off therapy appointments, and then I stopped going completely. I started keeping beer in the house, and told myself it was for the company I knew to be non-existent since I kept myself at arm's length from almost everyone since coming home. Jackie, Woody and Billy comprised the trifecta of relationships maintained in two years. Otherwise, I wallowed in my losses: Job. Identity. Wife.

At the core of everything, I missed being a cop. And working to find Bobbi Fisher—to at least find answers—seemed like real work. Cop work.

Bobbi Fisher was dead. No doubt about it. But I couldn't just come out and tell that to Mitch Fisher. He didn't want to hear that answer. I had nothing definite that said she was dead, outside of logic, intuition and fourteen years of cop experience.

What Mitch had, though, was hope. No matter what they

tell you, people always keep a little hope that a missing person is still alive. I'd seen parents keep bedrooms untouched years after a child went missing, pristine for that homecoming they told themselves was eventual. Stuffed animals unmoved. Posters for long-forgotten bands hung on the wall with yellowed Scotch tape. Life frozen and perfect in those rooms, like insects in amber, locking in grief, always delayed, always waiting.

I thought about Billy, and what it had been like when my mother didn't come home. I was young, and there wasn't much in the way of memories about it, just a day when she stopped being there. After the funeral, Billy took her clothes and bagged everything up and gave it to churches or to Goodwill. He never talked about her much afterwards. Photos disappeared from walls. It was like she'd been smoke, and a hard wind came and blew her away into nothingness.

So I would not begrudge Mitch Fisher for letting logic and good sense interfere with the fact that his sister was dead. But I still felt wrong, knowing this made me feel right somehow.

That's why I needed to get to Marlowe's early, to have an extra beer before talking to Doria Newland.

Doria walked in wearing a denim skirt a few inches above her knees, no hose, motorcycle boots and a leather jacket thrown on over a scoop-neck T-shirt that showed off her decolletage.

The bar was half-full, and most of those guys stopped to watch Doria walk through the joint. Toby Keith blared from the jukebox and the nightly news clattered along on the flat screen behind the counter, but no one paid attention to either. Doria was an interruption to clinking glasses and cigarette smoke.

She smiled and took a seat on the bar stool next to me and ordered a Killian's Red.

"You're punctual," she said.

"Technically, I was early," I said.

The bartender put Doria's beer on a napkin in front of her.

She drank some, a thin line of foam gathering on her upper lip. She licked it off

"You drink here much?" I said.

"Never been here before. Just drive by it on the way to work."

"Then why here?"

"No one I know drinks here, and the last thing I need in my life is people finding out I'm talking to you after hours."

"People saw us talking back on company time."

"Completely different," she said. "You talked to people and got nothing from it, because no one wants to tell you a truth today and have to empty their desks out tomorrow."

"You saying people kept things from the police about Bobbi?"

"There aren't secrets in offices, Henry. At best, you're not spreading the stories, and at worst, you're helping hide them." Doria shook a cigarette loose and lit it.

"Then what if we focus on the secrets involving Bobbi Fisher?" I said.

"Like I told you, Bobbi was looking for her white knight. She was young, cute, friendly, and she worked in an office full of old, ugly attorneys who think having money excuses their sins."

Doria drank beer, took a drag off of her cigarette. I caught myself watching her, how she moved. Nothing about her seemed self-conscious. She paid no mind to the guys staring at her, taking peeks between shots at the pool table or averting their interest from the weather guy with the hair plugs as he talked about the cold front coming in from the west.

"When she started at the firm," she said, "the lawyers hit on her, and she did her best to dodge 'em and keep everything professional. But they wear you down after a while, and she started seeing someone. And when I say 'seeing someone,' I mean 'fucking him.'"

"Who was the lucky winner?"

"Richard Walters, one of the junior partners."

"What can you tell me about him?"

"He's about fifty. Decent looking enough. Works out, so he's

31

not gone the all-gut-and-no-ass route. He's a good lawyer, kind of an asshole, but he's a lawyer, so that's a given, isn't it? And his wife's not bad, either. She's small-town hot. Dresses like the housewives from all of those shows, but she's got a good ass."

I raised an eyebrow. Doria smiled.

"What?" she said. "I can rut from the same trough as the rest of the pigs."

"You think Bobbi told herself Walters was in love with her?"

"You married, Henry?"

"That's a complicated question."

"Shouldn't be. It's like pregnancy or virginity; either you are or you're not."

"According to the law, I am, but we've been separated for a while."

"Any chance of reconciliation?"

"Maybe when the Browns win the Super Bowl."

Doria smiled. She had pronounced canines, almost like a vampire. "For women, and this may sound sexist or anti-feminist or some kind of '-ist,' but we enjoy having another person. You get kicked around enough, you learn there are worse things in the world than settling for whatever you can find. Sometimes something, as meaningless as it might be, is better than the nothing you're getting otherwise."

The bartender came by and asked if I wanted another. I hadn't realized I had finished it. I said no.

Doria reached out and touched the back of my hand. She kept it there, running a finger over my knuckles. She had a glint in her eyes.

"You hungry? I got steaks thawed out back at my house. I can throw 'em on the stove, do up potatoes in the microwave. Got a few cold beers, too."

I watched her hand as it crept up across the top of mine, eventually wrapping itself around my own. Her fingertips rubbed across my palm.

"I'm not sure me and another beer are such a good idea. I'm

not entirely confident of my ability to get home right now as is."

That smile on Doria's face lit up even brighter. "Honey, who said anything about you going home?"

I didn't know what to say on that. I couldn't remember the last time a woman had hit on me.

"I'm offering you my bed," she said. "No offense, but there are any number of guys in here who'll jump at the chance, and I can go somewhere else and find guys there too. So do you want to over-think this or you want to follow me home?"

I motioned for the bartender, slapped several bills onto the counter and walked out the door with Doria at my side.

Sleeping with Doria wasn't the best idea I ever had, but it had been so long since there'd been a second person in the room with me during sex, I didn't give a good goddamn about good or bad ideas. Even though I was rustier than a wagon left in the rain, and it wasn't quite the bullshit about never forgetting how to ride a bicycle, things fell into place well enough, and afterwards, as we laid there amid the smell of sweat and Doria's post-coital cigarette, I thought I'd acquitted myself well.

That was until somewhere in the recess of my brain I heard Maggie's voice. Saw her face. Imagined the scent of her perfume. That was all it took to drag me down my particular little rabbit hole of self-pity.

I rolled onto my side. Doria said something, but I pretended to be asleep, and soon enough I didn't have to pretend anymore.

CHAPTER 8

Coffee was brewing as I walked into the kitchen. Doria stood at the sink wearing a blue silk robe cinched at the waist, long enough to cover her ass, short enough to give an enticing hint of curve. She spun around with a large red coffee cup in each hand, cigarette hanging from her lips, a gray circle of smoke encircling her. She set the cups on the counter that separated the kitchen from the dining room and pulled the cigarette away and leaned across the bar to kiss me on the cheek.

"Mornin', sunshine," she said. She motioned toward the coffee pot at the end of the counter. "Got sugar there and milk in the refrigerator close to still being good."

I filled my cup and took a seat at the dining room table.

Doria dumped massive amounts of sugar and milk into her cup and poured in enough coffee to turn the whole mixture paper-bag brown before sitting down.

I stared at my coffee. I could feel her looking at me, waiting for me to say something.

"You mean to tell me this is where you get quiet on me, cowboy," she said.

"I'm out of practice," I said.

"Don't do many one-night stands?"

"I didn't know if this was a one-night stand."

She smiled. "What do you want it to be?"

I sipped my coffee. "You got an extra cigarette?"

34

She slid the pack in my direction. The picture on the front was an Indian wearing a headdress.

"American Spirit?" I said.

She shrugged. "They're all natural. They're supposed to be better for you. No rat shit and whatnot."

I lit the cigarette. "It's not like there's vitamin C in 'em. You'll still get lung cancer and die."

"I hope this isn't your idea of morning-after sweet talk, because you suck at it."

"Well, I'm a rock star at everything else."

She laughed. "You keep telling yourself that, cowboy. Tell me how it goes for you."

"Since I'm still here and you haven't thrown me out yet, it must be working out for me so far."

"I try not to throw my sexual partners out of the house until I finished my first cup of coffee." She drank her coffee, working hard to make an emphasis she'd reached the bottom. "And goddammit, it would seem that I just finished."

I took another drag from the cigarette before crushing it out. "A fellow can take a hint, don't you worry." I came to my feet. "I'll get dressed—"

Doria reached across the table and grabbed hold of my wrist. "Don't tell me you're this fucking stupid." She narrowed her eyes at me. "Honey, I'm forty. I've got a kid in college; ex-husbands I can sit down and hold conversations with without wanting to kill; seventeen months until I own this luxurious abode; and I'm waiting for that inevitable day where my tits sag so that my nipples point to my toes. When you put all of that in the mix, I possess neither the time nor the patience to bullshit. If you're so inclined, then sure, this can be two grown-ups doing grown-up things, or we can keep this keep talking and maybe bother to learn one another's middle name."

I couldn't act like it wasn't appealing. My ego and sense of self-worth had gone to shit in recent years, and there was something ego-affirming in a woman like Doria wanting me.

Doria's eyes went soft, and she smiled and said, "Whatcha thinking there, cowboy?"

I glanced at my watch. "I'm wondering what time it is you've got to be at work."

"And why are you wondering that?"

I smiled, and Doria nodded.

"I've got sick time," she said as she laced her fingers between mine and pulled me down the hall toward the bedroom.

CHAPTER 9

I was in the parking lot for McGinley and Kurt bright and early the next morning, drinking coffee and eating an egg and cheese biscuit from Tudor's. Tudor's, for the uninitiated, is a fast-food chain all across West Virginia, tasked with keeping Mountaineers fat and full of gravy, and our cholesterol high. It does its job well, with biscuits bigger than newborns. They are greasy little slices of heaven, wrapped in yellow paper that will forever stain any clothing it touches. They're extraordinary, and I recommend them highly should the opportunity arise.

I was working my way through this carb bomb I was calling breakfast when Richard Walters drove up in a red BMW convertible, looking every inch of a man who ruled his universe. I recognized him from his picture from the firm's website, discovered when I'd visited the local library to research him. I had spent an hour next to a sweaty fat guy wearing a T-shirt that may have once been white who was playing online poker and laughing to himself about jokes apparently only he got.

Walters had dark hair getting strategically gray, a December tan, and a thousand-dollar suit with a two-hundred-dollar tie. I hated him on sight. It may have been shallow of me, but I was okay with that.

I lacked for much in the way of options here. If I'd still been a cop, with a gun and a badge and a uniform, I'd have just shown up at Walters' office and laid the fear of God down on him and have made him tell me what he knew. I would have gone to a judge and subpoenaed phone records and emails, gotten search warrants, and made his life miserable to the point he'd have admitted he wore his wife's underwear to get me to go away.

But that wasn't an option. What I had come down to "Hey, let's go poke a badger with a stick." Which was fine since I wasn't much of a planner.

As Walters got out of his car, I wadded up the Tudor's wrapper and threw it on the floorboard with a dozen or so of its cousins, wiped the grease off of my mouth with a napkin, hopped from the Aztek, and crossed the parking lot in record time. Walters had just hit the door locks on his key fob before I was standing next to him.

He looked at me with the wide-eyed surprise of a person confronted with a clown coming out of a strip club. He took a step back. "Can I help you?"

I extended a hand and whipped out whatever charm I possessed. "Mr. Walters? My name's Henry Malone. I'm looking into Bobbi Fisher's disappearance. She's the young woman who used to work for you."

Walters turned on his own charm. It kicked my charm's ass. It was all smiles and bright eyes, and I bet he charmed the fuck out of little old women on jury duty. "Oh, that's right. I heard you came by the office the other day. How is the investigation going?"

"It's going. I'm following up on any leads."

"That's commendable of you, Mr. Malone. Must be hard, one man taking on a job where the state police failed."

"I wouldn't say they failed—"

"Did they find her and no one's shared the good news?"

"They have not, but—"

A smile. "In my line of work, when you don't do what you're getting paid to do, that's considered failure."

"Lucky for me, I'm not getting paid."

"You're doing this out of the goodness of your heart?"

"I'm hoping to earn a merit badge," I said. "I thought we could talk about Bobbi."

"If that's your desire, can I recommend you call my assistant and set up an appointment, and not come at me out of nowhere in our parking lot?"

"I understand that, Mr. Walters, and I appreciate your willingness to talk, though I'm wondering if when I make that appointment, should I mention to your secretary—sorry, your assistant—that you were fucking Bobbi Fisher?"

Walters' smiled cracked slightly, and his eyes narrowed. "I don't think I like what you're implying, Mr. Malone."

"I'm not implying anything," I said. "I'm flat-out stating you were banging Bobbi Fisher, and that seems like something people would want to know when they're looking for a missing woman."

All the practiced grace melted off of Walters' face like wax in July sun. His body tensed, and he moved forward, working to squeeze into my personal space. "What game are you playing, Malone?"

"No game," I said, trying to sound nonchalant. "But my guess would be the police would be interested, since they could see it as a factor in her disappearance."

When he smiled, it was all shiny white teeth, the sensation of a pure predator. "I give. I was fucking her. Good for you. Show me another attorney in this town who isn't fucking some piece of cracker cunt in his office. I was just unlucky enough that my slice of white trash ass got herself killed."

Walters adjusted his tie, grabbed his briefcase. "Find another way to spend your spare time, asshole. Build ships in bottles, or sew quilts. Whatever, so long as I don't see you again. If I do, I can guarantee you won't enjoy what happens next."

Walters walked away, heading into the law offices. Midway there, another attorney approached him, and he immediately shifted back to the consummate schmooze artist. Laughing and joking and unconcerned about me. The two men entertained each another as they headed into the building.

CHAPTER 10

My trailer rested on land Billy bought back in the sixties when he'd been a checkweighman and a union steward in the coal mines. The trailer was a doublewide I paid six grand cash for, a beat-up repo job with green algae creeping up the sides and windows with gaps I stuffed with newspaper to keep out the wind.

I didn't care, since I didn't do much in the way of entertaining, and just wanted a roof over my head. Billy offered to let me live with him when I came back; he owned a four-bedroom modular with a foundation, central air, and a satellite dish. I'd declined, because I didn't want to be the guy going back to live in his old room with Whitesnake posters still on the wall, and also because there was sufficient shame in moving back to Serenity. I could see his house from my living room window. That was enough.

I still dropped by a few nights a week, greeted at the door by the smell of fried potatoes and pinto beans, or beef stew and corn bread, meat loaf and green beans, and we'd eat together. Tonight it was country-fried steaks and mashed potatoes.

Billy manned the stove, wearing in a T-shirt, bleached blinding white, and blue jeans. He was seventy, still combing his hair with Wild Root, sporting a trimmed white mustache and thick black-framed glasses and a hearing aid. He was at fighting weight if seventy-year-old men were inclined to get into fights. He flipped the steaks one last time before pulling them off the skillet with a

41

fork, setting them on a piece of chipped dinnerware he and my mother bought with green stamps at the A&P, carrying them to the table.

I got a Coke out of the refrigerator and took a seat at the dining room table. It was the same table he had owned since I was a kid. I used to sit underneath it, playing astronaut while dinner cooked. On weekends my aunts and uncles and miners who worked with Billy would gather around the table and drink Pabst Blue Ribbon before it became a cool thing to do. They would play poker and listen to the country station out of Clarksburg since it was the only one that broadcast after midnight back then. The poker games were nickel and quarter bets, never anything serious, and sometimes they'd deal me in a few hands. I have more memories in my childhood of playing five-card draw with Billy than I do playing catch.

Billy set the plate on the table and walked into the living room and turned down the stereo where "Bitches Brew" blasted from vinyl on the same Montgomery Ward stereo that pre-dated my appearance into the world. Over time, I had nudged Billy to lay off the vinyl collection, all these LPs he'd accumulated over the years, first pressings of stuff from Van Morrison, the Rolling Stones, the Hollies, the Who, guys like that. My argument was that he should switch over to digital and save the albums since they would have been worth mucho dinero to the right folks.

"If I'm the one that owns them," he'd told me as he laid a needle to "Eat a Peach," "then I'm the person to figure out what they're worth, and they ain't worth anything if I can't listen to 'em. I already got 'em like this, so why spend money to buy 'em all over again?"

Once he was back at the table, he dumped food onto his plate, the chicken-fried steaks crispy and brown, the mashed potatoes nice and lumpy. He didn't make gravy, though, which seem like sacrilege to spare a meal like this a thick coating of peppery goodness. He said he never liked how he made it, that it had always been something Mom did better than him. I didn't argue the point with him; I fucking knew better.

I filled my plate, and we ate, not saying anything to one either, just shoveling food into our mouths and washing it down with our beverages of choice. Billy was drinking milk. Whole milk. Fuck fat and cholesterol; that was my father's credo.

I mentioned that Billy's my father, right? I mean, you're bright folks; I'm sure you'd figured that out by now. You didn't? Sorry about your fucking luck, then. I'll talk slower from now on.

Once we were finished and there was nothing left but dirty dishes, I gathered everything up and hand-washed it all in the sink as Billy sat at the table, chewing on a toothpick and reading the newspaper.

"Goddamn county commission wants to annex that land out by Denny Farmer's place," he grumbled as I rinsed soap off of the plates and set them in the drainer to dry. "Money-grubbing bastards, don't want nothing but being able to tax it. Fucking shame man works his whole life and all he's got to show for it is nothing but a bunch of bills and liens and papers from the bank."

Something new pissed him off every time he turned a page. The volunteer fire department had its hat in hand, asking for money for a new pumper truck. A group from out of town didn't think the school should have a live nativity scene. Churches were asking for donations to help during the holidays. None of it seemed to make Billy happy.

I dried my hands off and walked to Billy and patted him on the shoulder.

"I'm gonna go let Izzy out," I said. "Thanks for dinner. Good seeing you."

"Yeah, yeah," he said, shifting himself around and away from me as I headed for the door. "Good talking to you."

CHAPTER 11

I wanted to get drunk, but that was a shitty idea. I wanted to see Doria, and possibly get laid, and maybe that wasn't a hot idea either, but it seemed preferable to the options.

I chose to go back to my place, give Doria a call, check if she was busy. Izzy was asleep at the front door. I knew this because as I tried to open the door, I was met with a heavy thud and an unhappy grunt and the door only opened partway and I squeezed through the gap at the doorway to get in.

She didn't move when I walked in. If not for the snoring, I'd have thought she was dead. I crouched beside her and petted her on the head. Izzy was the world's shittiest watchdog, but she still was a better person than most people I knew. I'd gotten her from the shelter when I came back to Serenity. I'd been running low on things that loved me, and once I saw her, there wasn't a chance I was leaving without her.

I locked the door and walked into the kitchen.

A skinhead leaned against the sink, drinking one of my beers. He was tall, rail-thin, shaved head, a white V-neck T-shirt underneath a black jacket. The SS lightning bolt on his neck was fresh ink, gleaming in the kitchen light.

He didn't say anything, as though being in my house and drinking my beer was the most normal thing on earth. He took a long swallow and chucked the bottle at me.

I ducked to the right and dodged it, and then something hit

me from behind, right at the base of my skull, and everything turned deep and warm and black.

"This motherfucker's cable package ain't worth shit," someone said.

Someone else said something, but I couldn't understand what. I swam upstream through the murkiness of head trauma. What I heard resembled Neil Young feedback, with the occasional Lou Reed white noise thrown in for not-so-good measure. The black faded slowly, turning into a heavy haze, life viewed through cheesecloth. I made out the figure of a racist asshole on my couch, flipping through channels on my TV.

There was a shattering noise. I blinked and saw another shadow, on the farthest side of the living room, next to my record player. The tuning on my vision came through and there was another human shape, going through my record collection, removing albums from their sleeves and smashing them against the wall.

"Sorry, I don't have any Celine Dion, if that's what you're looking for." I was confident that was my voice just then. It surprised me until I realized it was an attempt to be a smart ass. Of course it had to be me.

The music critic ignored me, and took another LP and drove his knee through it, splitting it in half. The floor was littered with a dozen or more albums reduced to shards of black plastic.

"Nigger music," he said. He was working through the blues collection Billy had given me for Christmas a few years ago. First pressings from obscure Chicago labels, stuff that had long since gone out of print and would never find its way onto CDs.

He broke another album. "It's nothing but the corruption of true American music," he said. "Bluegrass, country. The music of white people. This shit here is nothing but ignorant nigger hollering."

I groaned. "If this is how this is going to go, knock me the fuck out again." I shook my head and immediately regretted it. I burped acid, and a twist pushed up from the bottom of my stomach. I cranked my head to the side and puked. I gagged and retched, and vomit dribbled down the side of my face.

I was flat on my back. I moved to right myself up and couldn't. The stink of puke, the warm slickness across my face, made me retch again, and I panicked, trying to sit up. They had tied my arms behind my back. I struggled to get free, and the bounds cut deeper into my wrists.

"Get him up before he chokes," the music critic said. The TV critic muttered something I didn't understand because I had a chunk of undigested dinner in one ear. There was a sudden jerk on the back of my shirt and a push and I was propped against the wall.

The TV critic, the one who had pulled me upright, was the one I'd caught in the kitchen. He stood over me with a dead-eyed look on his face, arms crossed over his chest. On the knuckles of one hand he had tattooed "SIEG." It didn't take a huge leap to figure out what was on the other hand.

The music critic glanced at me, gave a casual nod, and pulled out a Big Walter Horton album, sliding the vinyl out and twirling it between his index fingers as he crossed the room toward me.

This one was the obvious leader, older than the other one, somewhere in his thirties. He was beefier, and he'd let his hair grow enough that you couldn't see the fissures in his skull. He had a close-cropped beard and steel-toed boots with silver tips, straight-legged jeans and a black shirt buttoned to the collar.

"Lemme guess," I said to the music critic. "You're the brains of this operation." I glanced over at the TV critic. "Which must make you the ball sack."

The TV critic punched me. My head snapped at the blow. His knuckles slid across the puke on my cheek, and there was a cold comfort when he muttered "Motherfucker," and he tried to shake the vomit off.

Everything blurred for a moment, long enough that two

versions of the music critic wavered before me. He tapped the album gently against one leg.

"The fucker got vomit on me," the TV critic said.

"You punched him, Earl," the music critic said. "He had puke on his face. What the fuck did you expect would happen?"

I took a deep breath, accidentally sucking in a little bile. I tried to spit it out, but all it did was dribble down my chin.

"I hadn't planned company, or I'd have cleaned up the joint," I said. "Sorry to disappoint you gentlemen."

"You need better beer," Earl said.

"I'll hop right on that," I said. "I'd hate to think something displeased a connoisseur of the finer things in life like yourself."

Earl looked at the music critic. The music critic stared at me and said, "He's making fun of you."

Earl moved toward me and the music critic said, "Back off, Earl. You'll just get more puke on you."

"I'll hit him on the other side," he said.

"Not necessary," the music critic said, bringing his arm back and swinging wide and smashing the album across my face. The plastic shattered, and a dozen sharpened shards scrapped across my face. I closed my eye in time to feel one brush across my eyelid. Another caught underneath my eye and I felt the flesh rip and blood run down my cheek.

The music critic drove one of his silver-tipped boots into my side, right beneath my ribs. Air evacuated my lungs, and I pushed my head between my knees in time for whatever remained in my stomach to make a prompt, violent exit.

The music critic grabbed me by the hair and yanked my head back. I gasped for air as he crouched in front of me.

"You are fucking with shit that isn't your shit to fuck with," he said. "I'd recommend you back the fuck off and stay out of said shit."

I inhaled and exhaled, then spit in his face. He didn't blink, didn't change expressions, just keep looking at me, holding onto me as he pulled a handkerchief from a pocket and wiped his face off.

"This is the warning you get," he said. "There won't be a second. Understand?"

I swallowed and regretted it as the burn of acid ran down my throat.

"What d'you do to Izzy?" I said.

"What, faggot?" Earl said. Earl had gone back to the couch and had turned the TV to ESPN.

"Careful," I said. "You might see a black person. Hate for you to burn your corneas out."

"Nothin' but niggers on there anyway," he said, changing the channel. He hit a music station. Kanye and his ego swaggered on about something. Earl struggled to work a groove up, swaying back and forth to the beat.

The music critic turned and looked at Earl. "Turn that shit off now."

"But—"

"Now," he said. Earl clicked the power button on the remote, and the TV fell silent.

The music critic returned his attention to me. Lucky me.

"Is Izzy the dog?" he said.

"Yes."

"We did nothing to it. It was asleep when we got here."

"She."

"What?"

"'She.' She's a 'she,' not an 'it.'"

"Very well. She's never moved. I would never harm an animal."

"She's not your type anyway, I mean, if you hoped to ask her out."

He jerked my head and thumped it against the wall. Then, to throw a little accent mark onto things, he punched my knee. I screamed as the world flashed white with shock and pain. I sucked in air and prepared another wail as he shoved his handkerchief into my mouth.

I focused on breathing, pushing and pulling everything through my nostrils. I slammed myself around, tears welling in my eyes, straining to get my arms loose.

The music critic rose to his feet. I blinked through the tears and watched as he drew back a boot and slammed it into my chest. Ribs crack.

He stepped behind me and pulled a knife from inside his coat. There was a snap and then my arms hung free. The sensation of pins and needles ran from my shoulders to my fingertips as blood worked its way through. Not that I could do anything. Everything in my brain focused on me not shitting myself, or puking and choking to death.

"Come on," the music critic said. I turned my head away and pulled the handkerchief out of my mouth as they walked out of the room. The front door opened and closed.

I don't know how long I laid there, waiting for something to stop hurting. From the corner of my vision I saw something poke through the doorway. Izzy, sniffing, first at the puke, turning her nose at it, then walking over and licking my face.

I scratched her behind the ears. "You're the worst fucking watchdog ever," I said.

She licked me harder. It hurt like hell but I didn't make her stop.

CHAPTER 12

Woody said, "You look like a meat loaf."

"'An American Werewolf in London,'" I said.

"I'm not quoting the movie. This is a statement of fact. You look like the dinner special at Bob Evans."

The pool of people you can call after you get beaten up by white supremacists tends to be shallow. Woody was the only name on my list. He came over with a first aid kit and two cups of coffee from Sheetz.

We sat at my kitchen table as he wiped my face with peroxide. It burned, and I could hear it bubbling. I bit the inside of my cheek.

"Don't be a pussy," he said, pouring peroxide on a fresh cotton ball.

"It hurts," I said.

"Hey, I can leave and let you suture yourself up. I'm sure that would be interesting to see."

"Sorry if getting wailed on by neo-Nazis puts me in a foul humor."

"You sure they were skinheads, and not just the regular bigoted morons?"

"They seemed to speak the mono-syllabic language."

"Ten will get your twenty they're with the Brotherhood."

"The Brotherhood" was the National Brotherhood for the Advancement of European Heritage. That sounded somewhat official and prestigious if you weren't paying attention and didn't notice it was in reality nothing more than a bunch of white trash crackers with a two-hundred-acre compound in Parker County. The Brotherhood was the lynchpin for a network of so-called "white nationalist" groups claiming to be preparing for what it said was an inevitable race war. Mostly, though, they were a group of grade-school dropouts who liked owning guns and seeing how far they could push "open carry" laws by toting an assault rifle through Walmart.

"I'm seeing 'em in town more," Woody said. "Which is different. The Doctor used to keep everyone on the farm."

"I think we'll both agree the world's changed in recent years."

"The Doctor" was Doctor Frederick Randolph Mayhew, a debunked biologist from Idaho who'd established the Brotherhood after his university decided they didn't want faculty who claimed "the superiority of European genetics is blatantly obvious when compared to the mongrel nations of Africa." It must not have read well in the alumni newsletter.

Mayhew had passed on a decade prior from lung cancer, going to whatever white wonderland waited for him on the other side. Lacking unified leadership, the organization fell apart not long afterwards. Obama's first election fueled a resurgence, though, as your grandmother started spouting Kenyan conspiracy theories and coworkers shared email chains about FEMA death camps. Nothing seemed to make a certain class of cracker more nervous than his or her president being a guy who, a few decades back, you could have demanded move to the back of the bus.

No one was sure how many folks were on the compound. Mayhew had always prided himself on the group's self-sufficiency, staying off of the grid, raising its own food, all but declaring its sovereignty. Recently, though, more members were seen in town, playing the role of "good neighbor," buying groceries and seeing local doctors and working to integrate into the community. The Brotherhood hadn't gone so far as sponsor a Little League team, but hey, give it time.

All of that was easy enough to do when you considered that part of the reason Mayhew had chosen Parker County was because it was the least racially integrated county in all of West Virginia. Hell, society had already done all the work for them. I'd gone through twelve years of school without once ever knowing someone who was another skin color.

"What I want to know," Woody said, "was how you didn't know they were here. What'd they do, park and hike over here?"

Billy's property sat a quarter mile off the main road, up a paved road Billy had paid for himself since he said he didn't intend to bust a truck axle hauling ass up and down a gravel road. But it was Parker County, and hilly land surrounded damn near everything around you.

"That'd be my best guess," I said. "Not like it'd have been difficult."

Woody closed up the wounds on my face with a few stitches, wiped away the rest of the blood, and handed me my coffee. "So who you pissing off enough to bring the Brotherhood down on you?"

I told him about Bobbi Fisher. He listened and drank coffee and finally said, "Walters strike you as the kind to hang with the Brotherhood?"

"Wouldn't surprise me, but it doesn't feel like it's a match made in Heaven. The Brotherhood's more of a 'jackboots on the ground'-level organization, and I can't imagine Walters inviting them over to dinner. I doubt McGinley and Kurt would be happy if they had a white power fiend on the payroll, though."

"They wouldn't care if he was Jack the Ripper so long as he billed hours and didn't leave bloodstains on the furniture." He rested his elbows on the kitchen table. "You going to keep looking for her?"

"No reason not to, outside of common sense. My calendar is clear, and I don't take well to being told what to do."

Woody put away his medical supplies into a shaving bag. "While we're on the subject of what you should or shouldn't be doing, any reason you had beer in your refrigerator?"

"Kept it for company."

"You keep loaded guns for kids to play with, also?"

"Don't 'Big Book' me Woody. I'm not in the fucking mood for it."

"I won't thump on you, because it's plain you've had enough of that for the night. I will say you might not want to keep booze around the house unless you intend to drink again." He looked at me with one of those long, soul-searing looks I absolutely hated. "Are you drinking?"

It was hard to lie to a man who'd come over to my house and stitched up my wounds. But I did it anyway.

"No, I'm not," I said.

Woody nodded. "If you're saying you're not, then you're not." He motioned toward Izzy. Izzy was stretched out next to the table, face buried between her front paws, asleep. "How was she during all of this?"

"Grand. She slept through most of it."

"She might not be the best guard dog."

"No, but she's one hell of a doorstop."

Woody leaned over and rubbed her head. Izzy perked up, rolled her head upward and licked his hand.

He gave me a serious look. "You got a gun."

"An old .38. Keep it in my sock drawer."

Woody smiled. "I'm sorry, I meant a 'gun,' not some a pea-shooter." He rose to his feet. "I'll be right back."

Woody went out the front door. I sat at the table, feeling every hurt and pain my body had to offer. It was a staggeringly generous amount. I tried to imagine what sleep would be like that night, what just laying down would be like. My imagination wasn't good enough to picture it.

Woody walked in with a nine-millimeter pistol and a box of ammo. He set both on the table in front of me.

"A CZ-75," he said. "They made 'em in the Czech Republic. Sixteen shot magazine. Excellent stopping power."

It was heavier than I expected, and it caught me off guard and I fumbled with the weight.

"They're not the best concealed carry gun," he said, "but if you have it drawn and you shoot someone with it, they're stop moving, no questions asked." He stood up. "Come by the house and you can practice shooting it. Think you can manage to not get your ass kicked between now and then?"

"I'll do my best."

I walked Woody to the front porch and watched as he got in his car and drove away. Back in the kitchen I stared at the pistol. I stared at it until I got tired. That took ten seconds, tops. I double-checked the locks on the door, then realized the pair from the Brotherhood had gotten in despite the locks, so I jammed a kitchen chair underneath the doorknob until the door couldn't move, and I did the same to the back door, checked all the windows, and took Izzy and the gun to the bedroom.

Izzy sprawled out on the bed, slumping her fat head on the pillow next to mine. I loaded the pistol and set it on the nightstand next to the alarm clock and climbed underneath the covers with my clothes on. Everything ached, and what didn't ache didn't count, and I laid there for a while before exhaustion won over and I fell asleep.

CHAPTER 13

I invited Doria over to dinner the next night, an act of monumental stupidity since my abode reeked in both the literal and metaphorical sense of "brooding loner."

"I was wondering if you ever planned to call," she said when I answered.

"I was playing hard to get," I said.

"Don't. I don't like using my energy chasing something when I could use playing with what I catch."

Jesus Christ, but what the hell could I say to that?

I spent that afternoon cleaning and dusting and hiding all variety of sins, shoving things into closets and underneath the bed. I also dumped all the booze down the kitchen sink. I heard Woody's voice the entire time, sounding smug and superior and right.

This was all done between bouts of wanting to scream from pain and breaks to catch my breath. I popped Aleve along with the pills for my knee, and together they cut the edges off of everything enough to make life tolerable.

Doria showed up looking sexier than she had the night at the bar, dressed in jeans and an untucked man's dress shirt and a paper-thin blue cardigan sweater. Part of the sexiness was in knowing what was going on underneath the clothing.

She held a bottle of wine. "Thought it'd be nice to go with dinner." Then she caught sight of me. "What the hell happened to your face?"

"The Jehovah's Witnesses got mad when I wouldn't take their magazine," I said as I took the wine and kissed her.

Izzy walked up to Doria and pushed her face in hand. Doria laughed and rubbed on Izzy's head.

"Cute horse," she said.

"Thanks," I said. "That's Izzy. I plan to ride her into battle someday."

I don't possess a huge repertoire of cooking options, but I've got a few things I used to make regularly, back at a time I had shits to give. Weirdly enough, one of them was shrimp scampi, or at least my version of it, which was just sauteing shrimp in enough butter and garlic to stop a beating heart. The noodles were boiling, and I had just put the shrimp on as we walked into the kitchen. I took a wooden spatula and pushed the shrimp around the inside of the skillet while Doria rummaged through drawers.

"You have a bottle opener?" she said. "Open this bad boy up and let it breathe."

I pointed toward a drawer. She found the corkscrew and pulled the wine cork open with a "pop."

"What about wine glasses?"

"Somewhere," I said. "Most of my wine experience is with a screw-top lid, and those need little in the way of breathing or glasses."

She took two Mason jars I used as drinking glasses out of a cabinet. "A Boone's Farm man. I can appreciate that." She filled one glass and tipped the bottle to start the second when I said, "None for me, thanks."

Doria paused and looked at me. "Are you serious? Because if I drink this bottle by myself, I'm gonna look like a drunk, you know."

I kept my mouth shut and focused on the shrimp. The noodles finished boiling, so I dumped them into the colander in the sink.

Doria sipped wine and leaned against the refrigerator. "So

what's the situation with you and your little woman?" she said. "I mean, it's obvious she's never lived here, since no woman in her right mind would actively have anything to do with this place."

"I'll leave your comments with the decorator. And that seems like something of a trick question."

"Afraid you'll get caught up in the snare of a husband-hungry middle-aged cougar?" Doria said.

"I might not have used that exact phrasing, but it's close enough for government work, sure."

"Good. I'm not much for snares, though I've enjoyed the occasional four-point restraint."

"You do know the right thing to say to keep a boy's attention, Doria. It's an intriguing trait."

"'Intriguing' will do in a pinch. And I'm waiting on you to answer my question."

I added liquid to the shrimp. "We've been separated two years, and she still lives in Morgantown. We haven't seen each other in more than a year."

"Why aren't you divorced yet?"

"Because I haven't always been sure I wanted to be divorced. There's complicated feelings there. Maggie and I, we separated after I left the state police, and I started drinking too much. It'd been fine for years, because Maggie was a newspaper reporter, and those people can hold their booze, and she'd always been able to keep up with me, but it got to a point where she couldn't because I had nothing holding me back, so she kicked me out. That was my wake-up call, my 'bottom,' we say in meetings, and I spent a few months getting sober and I thought that would work and it didn't. She decided she was content without me, so I licked my wounds and came back to Serenity, because I had nowhere else to go."

I waited for Doria to say something. Izzy came into the room, looked at each of us, walked over to me and nudged my thigh with her head. I scratched at the top of her skull, and she pushed herself into me.

Doria finished her wine. "After all that, dinner had better be goddamn good."

Doria had a second glass of wine by the time we done eating, and I brought cheesecake and strawberries out of the refrigerator. She was halfway down a third glass, and I was having Coke.

I had set the dining room table, but Doria wanted to sit at the smaller kitchen table. Doria did a lot of the talking, about her daughter (Laura, a second-year med student at WVU) and her two exes (the first when she was right out of high school and three months pregnant, a messy nine-year thing fueled by the guilt and shame by two teens who didn't know better and became a pair of twenty-somethings who finally figured it out; the second was after she'd turned thirty-five and met a guy and decided she was afraid of being old and alone, then figured out two years in that being alone was better than killing the guy and dying in prison), and working at McGinley and Kurt ("scumbags and assholes almost the whole way around, and those are the ones I like").

She finished talking and said, "Do you still love her?"

"Maggie?"

She looked at Izzy, who was sleeping close to us. "No, the dog, you moron," she said. "Yes, Maggie. Your ex, or your current, or whatever you call her."

"I care about her. We had years together. That stuff doesn't just turn on and off."

"Does she want a divorce? Get to move on with her life?"

"She does."

"But you don't."

"I don't want the sense of failure," I said. "I don't like the thought I pushed her away, and I worked to do what I thought it took to get her back, but at the end of the day, none of that mattered."

"She's moved on, but you haven't," Doria said. "People

change, thank God. Maybe you both have a right to change, and not just you."

I nodded. "None of this is very appealing in a boyfriend, is it?"

Doria refilled her wineglass. "Honey, I haven't had a 'boyfriend' since I was eighteen years old. And not to ruin it for you, but you wouldn't be the first alcoholic emotional wreck I've made the beast with two backs with."

She walked around the table and pushed my chair back and sat on my lap, straddling her legs around me so she faced me and kissed me. Her breath was warm and sweet and I took all of it in as my hands slipped underneath her shirt, fingers finding their way to the clasp of her bra, snapping it open and setting her breasts free.

We almost fucked right there on the kitchen floor, because that's what people in movies do. That doesn't work for the folks with knee replacements who've had the shit beaten out of them, because it would not be hot when we got down on the floor and I couldn't get back up. Instead, we made our way to the bedroom. I turned the clock radio on to the John Lee Hooker CD inside, not that either of us paid much mind to the music. By then, it was only the rhythm that counted for anything.

She was gentle with me, knowing almost every inch of me ached. She lowered me onto the bed and undressed me and climbed on top and moved with the assurance and skill found only through years of practice. I almost felt like I didn't need to do anything, even as she orgasmed twice before I let loose, as she moaned and kissed me on the mouth.

Afterwards, lying in bed, I said, "Any reason you think Walters would hang out with white supremacists?"

Doria rolled over and propped her head up in her hand and said, "You really don't get this pillow-talk thing, do you?"

"I'm out of practice."

"No shit. But to answer your awkwardly timed question, I've

known Richard for years. He's many things, with 'asshole' and 'lying, conniving bastard' chief among them, but he never struck me as an out-and-out racist."

She took her cigarettes from her purse by the bed, wrapped the top sheet around her and went to the window, pushing it open and lighting up. She inhaled and blew a cloud of smoke out into the darkness.

"He makes the same comments that most guys around the office make," she said. "They never see a black man up close unless he's running defense for WVU, and they say they're not racist but they've got the answers for what's wrong with black people." She exhaled more smoke. "I doubt he's any more racist than the rest of the firm, which makes them the casually stupid most people are about the matter."

"Then why would Walters be associating with them?"

Doria laughed. "Why are you so sure it's because of him?"

I pointed to my swollen right eye and the stitches. "It's not like I owed cookie money to the world's most hostile Girl Scout troop. Those jokers made it clear I needed to not be trespassing into someone's affairs. Now because I tend toward being lazy, I don't play in other people's pools often, so it's not a huge leap that less than a day after I talk to Walters, I end up getting worked over by the Heckle and Jeckle of skinheads."

She finished her cigarette and closed the window and laid back down on the bed. The sheet slipped and exposed more of her. "A sane person would walk away from this."

I moved closer to her. Her body was soft and warm and I placed my hands on her hips and pulled her next to me. "Sane and I don't hang out together often."

"I suspected that," she said, leaning forward and kissing me.

CHAPTER 14

Directions to Woody's place involved the phrase "turn off the paved road." That's not uncommon in Parker County, but Woody's house was its own thing, where you came off the state road, then the county road, then onto a narrow one-lane dirt road, then cut down a gravel road that coasted to the end where an old farmhouse rested.

The house was original to the property, a two-story wooden construct with a front porch the size of some people's homes. Woody had kept up the house but had let the property go wild, with weeds and kudzu and wild grass swallowing up the acreage. All he kept clear was a few acres in back for his shooting range. That green was dead now, though, and the expanse of land brown and desolate. No place like home, I suppose.

As I pulled up, the front screen door opened and a half-dozen dogs rushed out in a flurry of barking and fur. One was a long-haired golden retriever, another was a boxer-pit bull mix, yet another might trace Dalmatian somewhere in its history, and the rest were a tangled mess of genetics too knotty for anyone to want to deal with. I counted a half-dozen as I got out of the car.

Only six meant Woody had downsized. He almost always had double that number of various and sundry hounds, ones he found wandering along the road or got dumped off somewhere close by. He kept the dogs long enough for them to become reacquainted with people and pack mentality and then found homes for them. When he didn't, those were a "foster fail," and they had a new home with him.

I asked Woody if he ever took in human strays. He said, "Normal conditions, you can rehab a dog. People, not so much. People got too many issues. When you realize that about a person, the most humane thing is to put them down where they stand."

Woody came out about two steps behind the dogs. His hair was in a loose ponytail, but he otherwise looked like a photocopy of every other time I'd ever seen him. His closet must have been a temple to simplicity.

I struggled to pet each dog amid the blinding flurry of affection as I worked the forty feet from the Aztek to the porch and tried to not get knocked down. Climbing the porch steps gave the same sense of satisfaction as the last forty feet of Kilimanjaro.

"I just put on a pot of coffee, if you want some," Woody said as I walked through the door.

"Two alcoholics drinking coffee," I said. "Who the fuck ever imagined of such a thing."

"Yeah," he said. "We should get a bunch of us together, have meetings, shit like that."

"Never work," I said as I followed him through the house.

"Probably right," he said as we walked into the kitchen. "Drunks are assholes."

The house was spartan, with basic Walmart furniture, nothing on the walls, an old tube TV on a stand in the living room, and a locked gun cabinet in every room. Oh, and the undeniable smell of dog. Because when you've got that many hounds running around, simple Febreze will not get the job done.

I took a seat at the kitchen table. "Everyone's an asshole. Drunks are just assholes who are, well, drunk."

Woody clattered a pair of mismatched coffee cups. Milk and sugar were already on the table. He filled the cups from a percolator on the stove.

I doubled the usual amount of sugar and milk I added for regular coffee and took a drink. It was like hot tar, except without subtlety and nuance. Woody took his coffee black.

"How you feel?" he said.

"I ache," I said.

"You look better. You still look like a fucking train wreck, but it's better in the margins." He sipped more of his coffee. "So, you wanna stop lying like a fucking pussy and tell me why you're drinking again?" He looked at me with flat eyes. "Anytime now."

I heaved a deep breath. "Okay, fuck, yeah. You're right."

"This I already knew. I want to know why."

"You know why."

"You're talking about excuses for why you drink. You line up twenty drunks and ask 'em why they drink, and the excuses will start sounding familiar about five in."

I stared at my coffee. "I should have expected that this was where we'd end up."

"Not really," he said. "I can shut up and we can go outside and we can shoot the holy hell out of shit if that's all you wanna do. All I'm doing is putting out there that whatever the hell your problem is, someday you might realize you're not a special fucking snowflake, you are not unique, and you're only as screwed up as the rest of us, so you can pull your head from whatever orifice it's resting in, see whether what you're doing is making your life any better, and consider what it is you need to do to make said life better." He finished the rest of his coffee in a long swig. "With that said, let's go shoot stuff."

There was a thirty-foot wide curved wall in Woody's backyard, constructed from old railroad ties, with human silhouette targets hanging from it. Woody had built it over a weekend, marking off the shooting distance himself, setting up the hay bales and creating a rather respectable DIY shooting range. I doubt he could have been more proud if the whole thing called him "Daddy."

Woody had two rifles slung over his shoulders, a .357

Magnum in a shoulder harness underneath his hoodie, a Glock
in a belt holster, and a .45 in the hoodie pocket. I had the nine
millimeter shoved into my back pocket, and my belt clenched so
the weight of the gun didn't drag my pants around my ankles.

The dogs opted to stay on the back porch; they were aware of
what was about to take place. On our way out I snapped up
shooting range earmuffs for us out of the living room gun cabinet
as Woody chose the rifles.

Woody set the rifles aside and took out the Glock and raised it
into position and took a firing stance. He shut one eye, leveled
the gun, and fired. Shots rang out quickly as spent cartridges
slung out of the weapon. He cleaned out the fifteen-shot magazine
in the time I took to exhale.

We circled the hay bales and inspected the target. I counted
all fifteen shots, and each one was a high-value hit. Five were
dead center bull's-eyes, the others grouped tight and not far off.
From the corner of my eye I saw Woody smiling.

"Show off," I said.

I blew through about a hundred rounds, some on my nine, others
on Woody's .357. We spent the afternoon in a haze of gun
smoke and the smell of cordite and said nothing else about me
drinking.

Back inside, as Woody made another pot of coffee, he said,
"You got a plan on this thing?"

"Piss people off until they do something stupid."

"That's a better constructed plan than what I expected,
coming from you."

"Thanks. Was awake all night coming up with it."

"The Brotherhood, they like to get on the news by stirring up
shit," he said. "Used to be the members made a big show with
guns and marches, but numbers were down for a long time, so
they've laid low a while. Maybe two of 'em went rouge and
they're freelancing out for Walters."

"If Walters was angry enough to send goons after me, might mean he knows something about Bobbi Fisher."

Woody poured coffee.

"You want some help?"

"I could always use the company," I said.

He nodded. "I get to control the radio, then."

CHAPTER 15

Woody liked National Public Radio, which meant we listened to "Fresh Air" while we sat in Woody's truck parked across from McGinley and Kurt. The host was talking Joyce Carol Oates, which seemed like a big deal to Woody. For me, it was like drinking NyQuil straight from the bottle.

"Who the hell is this?" I said.

Woody gave me a look like I'd just squat in the middle of Main Street to take a dump.

"Joyce Carol Oates?" he said. "Are you kidding me?"

"Don't give me shit about this, Woody. I'm asking a question here, that's all."

"You've never read Joyce Carol Oates?"

"I've never heard of Joyce Carol Oates, okay? If I'm asking who she is, why would I have read anything by her?"

Woody dragged his hand down his face. "She's one of the great living American writers. I...how in the hell have you never read Joyce Carol Oates."

"You keep saying all three parts of her name like it'll change something. You can just refer to her as 'Oates' now. We've established who she is." A beat. "She's not related to the guy from Hall and Oates, is she?"

"With God as my witness, Henry, if you're being serious, I will push you the fuck out of this truck and drive away. What was the last thing you read? For enjoyment?"

I thought it over for a moment. "Graffiti on a gas station bathroom wall the other day. Something about calling someone for a good time."

Woody returned his attention to the radio. I felt his scorn through the silence.

We had been sitting there since 7 a.m., watching the firm's employees shuffle their way into work. We listened to NPR to kill time, starting up the truck at regular intervals so the radio didn't drain the battery.

I volunteered to get coffee from the Tudor's down the street on a too-regular basis. Coffee on a two-man stakeout was a terrible idea, since it meant there would have to only be one of you left when the inevitable calls of nature rang and you had no other choice but to answer. But the trips were acts of self-preservation as we sat through a morning of news from places in Europe and Africa and South America I'd never heard of, followed by classical music. It seemed like a slow, painful death.

"You have no class," Woody said.

The comment caught me off-guard. "You really want to sell me on the idea that listening to this gives you class?"

"It's an indicator for your appreciation of culture, that you understand there's more going on in the world than what stops at the end of your nose."

"I have plenty of appreciation for culture. I watched a black-and-white movie last night."

"What was the movie?"

"*Pulp Fiction.*"

"*Pulp Fiction* is not a black-and-white movie."

"It is when Izzy falls asleep on the remote control and it screws up the menu settings so bad I can't get the color readjusted until the point that the one guy is butt-fucking the other guy."

"Let's go about this another way. Have you ever sat down with the intent to watch a black-and-white movie?"

"I have not, because they make color TVs."

"They've made color TVs the entire time you've been alive."

"My point. The world's never been black and white, so why would I want to watch movies intentionally in black and white?"

He shifted his body around to face me. "You're missing out on an entire kaleidoscope of cinematic history with one bone-headed statement."

"You can't call it kaleidoscope if it's not in color, can you?" I gestured through the window to the parking lot. "There he is."

Walters pulled into the lot in his BMW, sliding the car into his personal spot and getting out and heading into the building.

"He looks like an arrogant asshole," Woody said.

"He's a lawyer," I said.

"The terms aren't synonymous."

"I haven't seen that huge of a difference."

"I'm not sure how you're a more cynical prick that I am."

"Hours spent practicing when I should be reading."

"We all have to have our life skills."

"It was this or CPR." I shook my head. "Don't like touching other people's lips."

We kept on waiting, and the day kept on getting longer the more public radio we listened to. At noon a call-in show had a bunch of journalists talking about how Congress didn't doing anything useful or constructive, as if this was breaking news.

Lunch at Tudor's was a cheeseburger and fries and a twenty-minute piss thanks to the morning coffee. Woody took his break once I was back, and I scrambled to find anything else to listen to. An oldies station was doing lunchtime requests, so it leaned into too much AC/DC and Led Zeppelin for my taste, but at least I recognized it, and not droning eggheads chattering on about things I didn't care about.

Once Woody was back, the dial found its way back to NPR and the rest of the afternoon was spent on reports about terrible things happening in places I couldn't find on a map. It made me feel like an ugly American, and I didn't enjoy that. I'm not one to savor my ignorance, but I wasn't prepared to fix it, either.

By five, I was ready to go home. My body ached more than usual from being cramped in the truck all day. I wanted a drink, a pain pill, Doria to fuck me until my eyes rolled to the back of my head, or a combination of all three. I was daydreaming about this possibility when Woody's elbow jammed into my rib cage.

"He's leaving," he said.

Walters was part of a crowd of secretaries leaving the building. He looked like a sultan leading a harem. He got into his BMW, pulled out of the lot, and hustled onto the street.

"Shall we?" I said as I started the engine.

"Please," Woody said.

I kept several car lengths between us and Walters before we turned out into traffic and followed Walters.

Cop shows and movies make tailing someone look easy, that all you need to do is keep a distance and cross your fingers the person you're following doesn't catch on. That's bullshit. Your ideal situation for a tail is multiple anonymous-looking vehicles, picking up and dropping off the pursuit car.

But it was only Woody and me, and we'd opted to take his truck since my Aztek—the vehicle that killed Pontiac—looked like an escape pod from a shitty sci-fi flick, and Walters might have remembered it from the other morning. Woody's truck wasn't inconspicuous: a cherry red 1965 Ford pickup. But there were enough old pickups roaming Parker County, we figured it would blend better than my beast.

After five minutes cutting through Serenity streets, Walters led out of the city limits onto Route 485, a two-lane county road. This was our worst-case scenario. There was no other traffic and no way to hide.

A few minutes in, I realized Walters was following a car him-self: a later-model green Toyota that had been in the McGinley and Kurt parking lot. Woody and I had been so focused on Walters, we didn't notice the Toyota, and I bet the Toyota was why Walters hadn't noticed us.

It was just the three of us on Route 485 for ten minutes. We passed outlets for other small towns and communities, little strips of houses up narrow country roads.

The local no-tell motel appeared as we turned around a corner. The Jamaica Inn's reputation across four counties was for lax record keeping and a cash-only policy. It was the place to go if you wanted to carve off a slice of afternoon delight. That everyone knew about indicated there wasn't much real secret to it, but that's how small towns work: hide the secrets in plain sight and hope everyone is too polite to say anything.

The Toyota pulled into the lot, and Walters pulled in after it.

We drove another hundred yards, then cut a sharp U-turn and parked on the shoulder across the road from the motel. A well-shaped redhead, all hips and tits and va-va-voom, closed the driver side door on the Toyota and sashayed up an exterior flight of stairs. Walters came out of the motel office, twirling a key on one finger, and met the woman outside a room. They kissed as he unlocked the door and all but fell into the room.

Walters, it seemed, had moved on from Bobbi Fisher.

I called Doria on my cell.

"Hello, doll," she said.

I smiled, and my dick shifted in my boxers. I pushed back my prurient thoughts. "Question for you."

"Fire away."

"You got a redhead working at McGinley and Kurt?"

"Got a few. Why? You bored already?"

"Hardly." I described the woman Walters was probably using as a human trampoline at that moment.

"That's Kara Taylor. She's not been with the firm long. Why?"

"Followed her and Walters to a motel. I'm guessing he's showing her his legal briefs right now."

"Fuck." The way she said it, it sounded even more profane. There was further movement in my shorts. Goddammit.

"This a big deal?" I said.

"I wouldn't call it good. We shouldn't be blowing the bosses, but these girls get plowed more than an Iowa corn field. The best I can hope is she doesn't turn out like Bobbi."

I told her thanks and hung up. To Woody, I said, "Wanna foster chaos and create mayhem?"

"More than you could understand."

I told Woody what I had in mind. We got out of the truck and Woody opened the locked box in the truck bed.

I suppose I expected tools. Hammers, wrenches, screwdrivers, you know the drill. Hey, maybe even a drill. What I saw was a variety of semi-automatic weapons, cases of ammo, canister grenades, some double-bladed axes, and a sledgehammer.

I looked at Woody, my jaw slack. He stared into the truck box.

"Under most circumstances I don't even keep a sledgehammer," he said, "but I was helping someone in the program—"

"You have grenades," I said.

"I do." The way he said it, the "duh" was almost implicit.

I heaved a deep breath and reached in and took hold of the sledgehammer. "Let's do this."

I carried the sledgehammer as we crossed the road and walked to the motel. Woody had his cell phone out.

"I can't say this is the best idea I've heard," he said as we mounted the stairs to the second floor.

"You don't appreciate how bad my ideas can be. This one is 'Operation Overlord' compared to others I've had."

The weight of the sledgehammer compounded with my fucked-over knee to complicate carrying the damn thing up the stairs. I stopped halfway up and rested against the railing and took a breath. Sweat dripped into my eyes, and my chest felt like it weighed more than the sledgehammer.

"Need me to take that?" Woody asked.

I shook my head. The hell that would happen. Pride and

common sense were not about to barge their way into this party.

Outside of Walters' room, I pressed my ear against the door. There was much moaning going on inside.

Woody pulled a .45 from his hoodie pocket and held it in one hand and his phone in the other. I hoisted the sledgehammer as high as I could. My legs wobbled, and I braced myself.

"I don't think this was what Steve Jobs had in mind when they came up with camera phones," Woody said.

"I don't think Jobs did that," I said. "Invented camera phones."

"Are you sure? I was thinking—"

"We'll fucking Google it later. I can't hold this thing forever. On the count of three. One...two..."

"Three" did not happen. Gravity seized the sledgehammer and brought it down hard, knocking the doorknob off clean. I rammed the head of the sledgehammer into the deadbolt, and it gave way as the door splintered and came loose on the hinges. One more hit and the door flew open and Woody and I stepped into the room.

Walters was strapped down naked to the bed in four-point restraints, a zippered leather hood over his head. The redhead mounted him, wearing leather gear, a crop in one hand. Walters' chest was covered with a crisscross pattern of raised red welts.

Both turned and stared at us as we walked in. Woody fired off pictures with his camera. The woman sucked in air to let out a scream. I let the sledgehammer drop to the floor with a thud and rushed across the room. I took hold of her hand before she could take a swing at me with the crop. I put one hand over her mouth and bought the crop arm behind her back.

"It's fine," I said in my softest voice. "We're not here for you. You go, get dressed, and leave, okay? Put your clothes on and walk away and forget this ever happened. Understand?"

She nodded.

"Awesome," I said. "But I'm taking the crop from you first."

She nodded again, and her hand loosened its grip on the crop as I took hold of it.

"Outstanding." I let go of her.

She was early twenties, cute in a corn-fed way, with a spray of freckles across her face and a slight overbite. Tears welled in the corners of her eyes.

"Just go on," I said.

Her clothes were in a pile at the foot of the bed. She threw them on—a sweater and a long skirt—over the leather outfit, grabbed her purse, and headed for the door.

Woody nodded as she walked by. "Drive safe," he said.

I looked at Walters. The zipper was closed over the mouth in the mask. He wanted to scream, but the noise came out muffled and meaningless.

Woody shoved the pistol into the back of his jeans. "We've gotta show his face to make these pictures count for anything," he said. He glanced at the door, barely hanging onto the frame. "And I'm sure this ruckus we raised didn't go unnoticed."

I soaked a washcloth in the bathroom sink and brought it back. I reached for the hood zipper and Walters whipped his head away and growled.

I took a deep breath and climbed onto the bed. I dropped to my knees, pinning Walters' shoulders to the mattress. The impact sent waves of pain through my body, and I wasn't real fond of how close my junk was to the head of a man in a zippered hood, but the action caught him off-guard long enough to let me yank the hood off and shove the washcloth in his mouth.

Walters' eyes were wild and angry, his face flush. I hopped off the bed and Woody stepped over and took fired off about a dozen photos on his phone.

"Got 'em?" I said.

Woody nodded. "You wanna pull your dick out, put it next to his face, make it look a little gay?"

"I think we'll call this good."

"Your call, man."

I sat on the edge of the bed. Walters' restraints were Velcro straps, and they looked cheap. That was disappointing somehow. You drive the car that Walters drove, dressed the way he dressed, you'd think you'd throw a little extra cash into your kinks.

"This is an interesting look for you," I said to Walters. "You should try it in court, just for shits and giggles."

Walters strained to move. There was the rip of the Velcro coming loose.

I patted him on the face. "Just so you know, I'll keep on looking for Bobbi. Send your little Nazi buddies after me again, and those pictures go to any living soul who might ever care. I'll email them to TV stations, other law firms, your wife, your mother, your second-grade teacher, the girl you fucked after your senior prom. And if you had anything to do with Bobbi disappearing, I'll bury you. Are we clear?"

Walters was silent. He couldn't have said much anyway, but you get the point. Instead, he stared at me with furious eyes.

"Good," I said. "As long as we understand one another."

Woody and I left the room, and Walters screamed as we walked out the door. A fat middle-aged guy who looked like motel staff came up the stairs and pointed at us.

"Hey! Hey you!" he said.

We stopped. "Yeah?" I said.

He glanced inside Walters' room, then looked at us with unrestrained boredom. This wasn't the first time he'd seen a half-naked man in restraints.

"What the fuck happened here?" he said.

"He needed towels," I said before we walked away.

CHAPTER 16

The pounding on my front door woke me up the next morning. I'd fallen asleep on the couch watching a movie I couldn't remember, and I was confused and sore as I peeled my eyes open and rays of December sunshine cut slits through the blinds. Izzy's head rested in my lap like a bowling ball. I pushed her off of me and shook my leg around to stir blood flow before going to the door, dragging my foot behind me as sensation returned to it.

The Parker County sheriff's deputy standing at my door was about six-four, wearing a sheriff's department jacket over a pale blue departmental polo shirt. His thick neck strained the opening on the shirt, and his blond hair was shaved close enough to let his scalp to shine in the sunlight. His hands rested on his gun belt. He didn't smile.

"Henry Malone?" he said.

"I feel as if there's no right answer for that question."

"I'm supposed to bring you in, have you talk to Sheriff Simms."

"Am I under arrest?"

"Should you be?"

The correct answer for that was "yes," but it didn't seem the prudent way to go.

"Any reason the sheriff wants to talk?" I said.

"That's a matter for you and him to talk about, not you and me."

I looked at my watch. It was just after eight. "Early in the day, isn't it?"

"Not really. Lots of folks already at work. I'm working already."

I stretched, and things popped that shouldn't have popped. "Got an objection if I shower first?"

"You gonna try to climb out the window or nothing, are you?"

"You wanna sit on the toilet and watch while I'm in there?"

"I do not."

I stepped aside to let him in. He had to angle to get his shoulders through the doorframe.

"I can make coffee," I said. "You're welcome to help yourself while I wash off my sins."

Izzy walked into the hallway. The deputy stopped when he saw her. Izzy chose that moment to yawn. It was like staring into the gaping maw of a hippo.

"Big dog," the deputy said. He hesitated, staying close to the door. "He bite?"

"No, she doesn't. You may drown from the drool, though. And you're the second person to call her 'he.' Does she not look feminine?"

The deputy stared at Izzy. "She looks like something parents should pay a quarter so the kids ride at the county fair."

I started the coffee as the deputy took a seat at the table. Izzy walked over and laid at his feet. He looked at her as if he expected her to rip his throat out.

"The worst that'll happen is her snoring might rattle your fillings loose," I said as I headed to the bathroom.

His name was Carl Thompson, and he was the chief deputy and had been since leaving the state police a decade earlier, stationed around Bluefield, in the southern coalfield region of West By God. He told me this as we drove to Serenity, to the county courthouse where the sheriff's office was. I sat in the back of the cruiser and listened and watched the road pass by as he drove.

The Parker County Courthouse was a limestone building dated from 1892, listed on the National Registry of Historical Places, complete with a brass plaque out front that said so. We got there a little after nine, once I'd showered and scraped off two days' worth of beard and we'd each had a cup of coffee. By then, Izzy was sitting next to Thompson, and he was hand-feeding her treats.

The sheriff's office was on the third floor. Thompson led me in and sat me down in a visitor's chair in front of the desk.

The HVAC system was working overtime; the office was hotter than an asshole in Hell, and I took my coat off while I waited. Thompson leaned against the wall behind me and remained as wordless as a statue.

After a half-hour of utter silence, the office door opened, and the sheriff stepped in. Sheriff Matt Simms was younger than I expected: early forties, a little heavy, dark hair flecked with gray, dressed in a blue denim button-down shirt with a sheriff's department logo where a pocket would have been, tan Dickies and a department-issued .45 in a belt holster. He smiled and shook my hand before sitting down behind his desk.

"How are we today, Mr. Malone?" he said.

"I don't know how 'we' are, but I'm sleepy, sore, horny, and curious why the sheriff dragged me to his office on a random Wednesday morning."

"I could have done without the 'horny' part, and it's Tuesday, Mr. Malone."

"I'm lousy with dates," I said. "Not that I don't appreciate getting woken up by Grape Ape back here."

Simms leaned back in his chair. "I took time to check into you, Mr. Malone. Shame about what happened when you were a trooper. An incident like that, you could have stayed on with the state police, you know."

"I got offered something in an office."

"Which wasn't your style."

"It wasn't."

Simms nodded again. He looked contemplative. Or consti-
pated. Something. I wasn't sure what. "Did you need to go
busting up that motel yesterday?"

"'Need' and 'want' are sometimes indistinguishable things,
Sheriff. What I needed was to have Richard Walters not send
people to kick my ass, and it seemed a way to get that point
across to him."

"And you succeeded there, let me tell you, because last night
I got a phone call—"

I buried my face in my hands. "Holy fuck, please say this
isn't when you tell me what an important man Walters is, and
how he's got sway in the department, because—"

Thompson's rough knuckles dug into my neck, and he had a
firm grip on my shirt collar, tightening it around my throat.

"Men don't talk when other men speak," Thompson said in
a low monotone. "It's just good manners."

I choked against the neck of my shirt. "Sure thing, Quiet
Riot," I said with a gasp.

Simms gestured his chin toward Thompson, and Thompson
let me go.

"Mind if I continue?" Simms said.

I got some air and rubbed at my neck and pulled at my collar.
"I'm sure as hell not going to stop you."

"Thanks. And no, that's not the case at all. Walters is a
prick, and the only weight he pulls is because of McGinley and
Kurt; they bring a lot of money into the county. No, the phone
call I got last night was from my ex-wife, who for reasons I'll
never quite fathom, opted to marry Richard Walters."

Simms stood and walked to the window and pushed it open.
A crisp breeze blew into the room. He sat in the windowsill,
taking up most of the cool air, though some still made its way
in toward me.

"The problem is, I want her happy," Simms said, "and I
suppose that being with him makes her happy. So once the motel

called us and Carl showed up and found Walters strapped to the bed—and once Carl got done laughing his ass off, I'll add—Walters told Rachel, my ex-wife, that he'd been meeting a client at the motel when you showed up, harassing him. Rachel's got a huge heart, and that heart takes up blood flow that should go to her brain, I guess, because she believed him, which is why she called me, angry that you're causing him issues where there shouldn't be. To make her happy, I agreed that I'd have a talk with you about the matter."

"She know about Walters' tendencies to fuck around?"

"No. Rachel always wants to think the best about people, and I won't spoil that about her."

"There're pictures of him strapped down to that bed. You getting them, that's easily arranged."

Simms shook his head. "Rachel and I, we separated on not-the-best terms, and that's my fault. She's the sort to dig her heels in deeper and try to make things work, regardless of what kind of asshole Walters is."

"So since you and he are buddy-buddy, maybe you can tell me if it's conceivable Walters is involved with the National Brotherhood," I said.

Simms raised an eyebrow. "I don't, but you have aroused my curiosity now."

I told him about Mitch Fisher asking me to look for his sister, and everything that had happened so far, including the beat down by the skinheads. At the rate I was telling the story, it would make the newspaper, and Billy would have something new to complain about.

"I doubt Walters is a bigot," Simms said. "Walters is a scumbag who wouldn't care who showed up at his office door so long as they had a cashier's check for the retainer. On the question of the skinheads, however, I have a fair idea who one of the two guys would be." He sat back behind his desk, scribbled something on a scratch pad, tore the sheet off, and slid it across the desk. It was a name—Earl Teller—and a local address. "I'll bet that's the kid. Teller's not what you'd call a 'deep thinker.' Used to have dealings with him, juvie type stuff, and he kind of fell into the Brotherhood several years back."

I folded the paper and put it in my coat pocket. "What do you suppose will happen if I find out Walters is attached to the Brotherhood?"

"Hell if I know," Simms said. "Maybe people won't care. Maybe they will. Most folks don't seem to mind the Brotherhood much so long as they mind their own business."

I pointed at Simms. "But what about you?"

"Me? I wouldn't give a shit if the whole compound blew up. They're an annoyance whenever a news show comes to town, wants to explore 'hate in small-town America' or whatever they're blathering about, and traffic gets tied up for a week. Plus, I'm not a fan of the narrow-minded and willfully ignorant. They give the good people of this county a bad name."

I shook my head. "Lofty as that speech was, I more meant what happens for you? You think you can win your wife back with this?"

Simms' expression soured, as if he'd been crop-dusted in a grocery store aisle. He pivoted around in his chair to stare out the window. "Carl, can you drive Mr. Malone back home?'

Thompson placed one of those baseball mitts he claimed to be a hand on my shoulder. "Sure thing, Sheriff."

I shrugged. "Guess it's my time to go then."

Still with his back to me, Simms said, "Guess it is."

CHAPTER 17

Woody and I found Earl Teller at his house, laying underneath a car on blocks, fiddling away on it, stopping occasionally to drink a beer. It was about nine in the morning. We were in Woody's pickup, parked down the block from Teller's house.

"Think this kid knows anything?" Woody said.

"I doubt he knows not to stare at the sun, but he's what we've got," I said. I looked over at Woody. "What d'you do before you did whatever it is you do now?"

"Things."

"That's vague. Narrow things down?"

"Different things."

"Thanks for clearing it up. Were you a cop?"

"Does it matter?"

"I'm curious. You owning an arsenal isn't all odd. Owning canister grenades could be seen as slightly unusual. Also slightly illegal." I tapped fingers across the dashboard. "You've been my sponsor a while, and I realized I don't know much about you."

"You never asked," he said. "You knew enough, you asked for help."

"Yeah, but I'm a dumbass. Didn't have anyone else to call."

"This isn't making me feel sparkly, Henry."

"I suppose I thought maybe knowing something about you might be good."

"I don't do touchy-feely, Henry. I'm your sponsor, and

apparently I'm your sidekick. You want more than that, call your therapist."

Then he turned up the radio.

Woody and I didn't say much to one another the rest of the day. Teller went and hung out at someone's house for the afternoon. About three in the afternoon, Teller left and drove to Browne's Hardware on Miller Street. The faded and chipped letters on the storefront sign proclaimed "Established 1947."

We parked and watched Teller go inside.

"Old Man Browne," Woody said. "Bennett Browne. His dad owned the store when it started, and Browne's run it since the seventies. Son decided he didn't want the place, but he went to WVU, got a civil engineering degree, moved to Pennsylvania, left Old Man Browne to keep plugging away, showing up every day."

I remembered the store. Billy used to go there all the time when I was growing up, getting pipe or soldering supplies. I wasn't a kid with much curiosity in anything like that, though, so Billy's efforts to teach me something were met with disinterest at best, abject failure at worst.

A few minutes passed and Teller walked out, a large box under his arm. He dumped it into the back of his car and drove off.

Teller made three more stops—another hardware store, and two pharmacies—and came out a few minutes later each time, carrying big boxes or bags each time. By then the sun was setting and streetlights were coming on and businesses in Serenity were hanging up the "Closed" signs. Teller headed home, and we followed.

"Hardware stores and pharmacies," Woody said.

"I doubt Teller has either an interest in home improvement or the world's worst allergies, which leaves another possibility, doesn't it?"

"It does."

"That possibility being our boy is farming the ingredients to cook meth."

Woody nodded. "They grow up so fast these days."

"And they're so fucking stupid when they do."

CHAPTER 18

Doria pulled her car up next to mine, cop-style, driver's side to driver's side. We were in the Walmart parking lot outside the town limits. I was drinking coffee and eating a burrito I'd nuked in the microwave at One Stop before driving over.

"That's disgusting," she said, wrinkling her nose at the burrito.

"You smoke," I said. "This is worse?"

"You smoke too."

"I'm not a hypocrite about it."

"Calling me out on hypocrisy won't earn your way back into my lacy underthings, so you know."

"Understood. How's things in the office?"

"Glorious and boring, Alice. Walters didn't bother to show up yesterday and dragged in late today. There're whisperings that the other partners aren't real happy with him."

"Good."

"Good for you; for the rest of us, not so much. Lawyers are crabby, ungrateful fucktards on good days. When someone slaps them on the wrist, they get pissy."

I took a bite of the burrito. Solid ice. "Fuck this," I said, and chucked the rest out onto the parking lot.

"You're littering," she said.

"It'll bio-degrade." A beat. "Eventually."

"That thing will outlive cockroaches and Keith Richards in the nuclear apocalypse."

"Haven't you heard? Nukes are out. The apocalypse will be all about zombies."

I looked toward the Walmart entrance. A woman in stretch pants warped to the fabric's limit rode a motorized shopping cart out of the store. Her basket overflowed with snack cakes, frozen pizzas and Mountain Dew.

"You think Walters killed Bobbi?" Doria said. "Or had her killed?"

"No clue," I said. "But I figure I'll keep poking around until something happens. Folks might not be happy with me and that could bounce back on you, if they connect us. These guys, they're not afraid to get physical."

Doria reached into her glove compartment and produced a semiautomatic pistol. Out of her purse she brought a snub-nosed revolver. She pointed at the semiautomatic. "This is the one I keep in the car," she said. She gestured to the revolver. "That one lives in my purse. And not that you looked, but I've got a few others at my place, so if someone shows up and they want to cause trouble, them trying to get physical won't be an issue. While we're on the subject of getting physical, when do I get to see you again?"

"When would you like to?"

"Tonight? If you'd like that."

"I'd like that. Can I call you?"

"Works better than sending me a letter. Let's do my place. Your crib is too much like a dorm at the saddest college ever." She smiled and started up the engine, rolled up the window, blew me a kiss and drove off.

I sat there. "Gal's got an arsenal," I said to myself. "Why's everyone got more guns than me?" My knee chose that moment to throb, a kicking answer to my question.

"Point taken," I said, and pulled out of the parking lot.

CHAPTER 19

Teller got an early start to his day; he picked up his supplies from the pharmacies and hardware stores then drove to Sheetz and headed inside. We followed him, because we didn't have much else to do, and parked outside.

Woody reached under his hoodie and brought out a Sig Sauer. "You carrying?"

I had the gun Woody had given me in my coat pocket. It was heavy and awkward, and I hoped I didn't have to use the damn thing, but I sure as hell wasn't going anywhere without it these days.

Woody put his gun back in his hoodie pocket and opened his door. "Come on," he said. I followed him to Teller's car. He leaned against the hood and rested a foot on the bumper.

Teller came walking out with a "don't give a fuck" strut, lighting a cigarette and cradling a twelve-pack of Natural Light. He snarled at the sight of us.

"Get off my car, fuckers." He looked at me and a dim light of recognition flashed behind his eyes. "I remember you. What you want, faggot?"

Woody smiled and looked at me. "Tough guy."

"Balls made of marble, I bet," I said.

Teller took a deep drag off his cigarette. "You cocksuckers need to get off my ride and haul your fag asses back to wherever you came from." He gestured toward me with his cigarette.

"Done kicked your ass once. I got no problem doing it again."

"I wouldn't say it was a fair ass kicking," I said. "Clubbed me upside the head, tied me up, bitched about my beer and my cable. Besides, it was two of you, and only one of me." I motioned toward Woody. "You didn't beat him up."

Teller smiled, and the cigarette angled upward between his lips. "Whatever, faggots." He spit the cigarette out, set the beer on the ground, pointed at Woody. "I'm gonna fuck you up." Pointed at me. "Then I'm gonna fuck you up." He smiled again, a mouthful of yellow teeth. "Then I'm gonna find your mom, and I'm gonna fuck her in the ass, because that's how she likes it." He rolled his shoulders back, twisted his head until his neck cracked, cranked his body toward Woody, and put up his fists. "You first, fucker."

"Sure thing, sport." Woody pushed himself off of the hood of the car, unzipped his jacket, and let swing a right hook that caught Teller in the jaw. Teller's head snapped and his body whipped back "Matrix"-style. He spun on his toes like a balle-rina and face-planted on the pavement.

Woody patted Teller down and tossed a set of car keys to me. "You drive his," he said as he hoisted Teller over his shoulder and carried him toward his truck. "Follow me."

Woody threw the bucket of water on Teller. Teller snapped back to the real world with a start and a scream, followed by the realization that he was naked and handcuffed to a flagpole. We were outside Woody's house; I shivered under my coat. The temperature was dropping and snow was sputtering from the sky.

"See," Woody said. "I told you he wasn't dead."

Teller was so skinny, he hurt to look at, his sinewy body covered in bad Nazi ink. There were swastikas and more SS lightning bolts, the death's head, an assortment of runes. Along the left side of his rib cage in someone's piss-poor excuse for handwriting, was "We must secure the existence of our people,

87

and a future for White Children." Underneath that was "14/88."

He banged at the flagpole with the handcuffs. "You faggots get me the fuck off of here," he said. "Let me go or I'm coming back here with my white brothers and we'll fucking destroy you."

"Uh huh," I said. "Asshole, you've got no negotiation room here. You, or that shriveled up roll of dimes you call a dick."

He curled his lip back. If he thought it made him seem tough, he was wrong in many, many ways. "This some queer sex shit? Fucking faggots. You think ass-fucking me gonna make me one of you?" His gaze whipped back and forth between Woody and I. "This is an AIDS thing, ain't it?"

I open-palm smacked him upside the head. "Teller, if we were gay, do you think you'd be our first choice? No one in his right mind would put his dick anywhere near that pathetic shit-chute you call an ass."

His teeth chattered an insane, uneven rhythm, and his body convulsed as a wave of cold rolled over him. He closed his eyes and sucked in some breaths. "What do you want then?" he said as he calmed down.

"Answers."

He steeled his face up into grade-school stoicism. "My name is Earl Teller, a blood member of the National Brotherhood for the Advancement of European Heritage. I have sworn an oath to follow to the death the pledge of the 14 Words—"

"Oh fuck this." I stood up and said to Woody, "Have at him."

"With pleasure," Woody said. He raised the water hose and opened up the spray. The water shot straight into Teller's face, and he tried to scream, but he choked and gagged as the stream caught in the throat.

I let it carry on for a few seconds, enough to scare Teller, before I made a slashing motion across my throat and Woody cut off the water. Teller shivered and pulled at the cuffs and flung himself around wildly. I figured he'd be stupid enough to dislocate his shoulder.

"I want to know about what's going on with the stores in town," I said.

Teller looked at me with dead, empty eyes. "The National Brotherhood for the Advancement of European Heritage has sworn to uphold and protect the ideals of the natural superiority of the white race, and as such—"

"Hit him again," I said.

Woody opened up the hose on Teller. It was longer this time, and Teller's body spun and tried to get away from the water and couldn't.

Once Woody had turned the water off again, I said to Teller, "We've got nothing else to do today, and hypothermia's not out of the question if you wanna keep up your 'white power brotherhood' bullshit, so it'd be in your best interest to answer a few questions for us."

Something that might have been intelligence shone in his eyes. Synapses dormant for years sparked for a moment, and then the moment was gone, replaced by the look of a wild animal, acting on instinct.

"The National Brotherhood—" he said.

I heaved a sigh. "Do it."

Woody opened the nozzle full blast. Spray misted toward me, and it felt like needles against the exposed skin of my face. I couldn't imagine what it was like on Teller. I didn't want to, either.

Woody stepped closer toward Teller, and the force of the water hit Teller harder. Woody angled the hose up to catch Teller in the face. Teller struggled to pull away from the stream, and fear registered on his face. Legitimate fear. That fear that people get when they realize how deep the shit is that they're standing in, and somewhere I saw that Teller thought he might die today.

I looked to Woody. "Shut it off." Woody took another step forward. Teller's body vibrated, and he wrenched himself in different directions, his body contorting itself in painful positions.

The handcuffs clanged against the pole like a fire alarm bell, and Teller's sinews stretched and popped in his arms. Blood dripped from his wrists, mixing into the water pooling around him.

I smacked Woody across the shoulder.

"Goddammit, I said to shut it off," I said.

Woody turned the water off. His mouth did that almost-smile thing. "Sure thing," he said.

Teller shivered uncontrollably, and his teeth chattered so hard they might crumble to pieces.

I crouched back next to him. I said to him, "You wanna try this one more time?"

He sucked in air through his nose. "I'll tell you, I'll tell you, just so long as you don't fucking spray me again. Okay?"

"Talk."

He sighed. "The stores, they're giving us the shit, and we take it and make meth." He hit me with a look that was equal shares hatred and exhaustion and fear. "Now let me the fuck go."

"Good lad." I smacked him lightly on the cheek. His skin felt like a slab of fresh fish. "See how simple that was?"

We cuffed Teller's hands behind his back, and we kept him naked since he seemed less likely to do anything stupid that way, but we took him inside and draped a blanket over him and let him sit on the living room couch once Woody had put towels down.

Woody and I drank coffee. Steam rolled out of the cup and Teller eyed it with envy.

"How'd it get started?" I said.

Teller might have shrugged; he was shaking so hard it was difficult to be certain. "Don't know. I got told to pick up supplies from these places two or three times a week, and that was it."

"That National Brotherhood bullshit about 'purity of body and spirit,' how's that fit into this?" I said.

He looked at me. "I do what I'm told. They said to make

these pickups, and it's what I do. You live here, watch the news, see how people are, how they live. Meth makes money, it's that simple. We make the shit and sell it to the mongrels and the race-mixers, and they eat it up. We can't make enough."

Earl Teller was a charmer, I had to give him that.

I drank more coffee. "What about Walters? How's he fit into this?"

Teller shrugged. "Fuck if I know. I do what I get told to do, that's all." He shrugged again. "I'm cold."

"I bet you are. And my face hurts where you and your buddy tried to loosen my teeth. Pain is part of life, ain't it?"

Teller stared at the ground. "Wasn't nothing personal. I got told to get you to leave the lawyer alone."

"And you never thought to ask why?"

"I'm a sworn blood member of the Brotherhood and a soldier in the army to keep the white race free. I'm not in the 'asking questions' part of shit. I'm in the 'getting shit done' part of shit."

Woody laughed this time. "That makes you a bitch then, right?" He came up out of his chair and went halfway across the room and looked at Teller. Teller puffed his chest out, a small bird trying to make himself seem bigger, tougher. "That's all you are, is a bitch. You're the bitch boy for a goddamned brotherhood—" Woody tossed air quotes around "brother-hood" "—of bigots, rednecks and crackers."

Teller curled back his lips to show his teeth. "The Brother-hood is the only hope our race has. While the niggers and Jews and sand monkeys are out there blowing up the society white Christian people built, the Brotherhood is working to preserve what we have, what we created. These niggers—"

Woody slapped him, and Teller's head snapped back hard. Much harder and it would have spun a full three-sixty. Teller's tongue flicked out, tasting the blood dripping from the corner of his mouth.

Woody clinched his hand into a fist. "Use that word one

more time, or another one like it, and I'll throw you in a hole in the backyard, but I'll make sure you're still breathing when those first shovels of dirt hit you." To me, he said, "Get his clothes back on him and let's get him back to whatever hole he crawled out from. I'm tired of looking at him."

I'm not sure who was more scared shitless of Woody: Teller, or me. My sphincter pulled so tight it wouldn't let a whisper of air pass, though.

"Agreed, but one last thing for Einstein here," I said. "The other goon with you; who was he?"

Teller slumped his body inward and ducked his head, as if embarrassed, as if he had the capacity for embarrassment. He said something so quiet, a mouse farting on a cotton ball would have drowned it out. I leaned in closer.

"Repeat that," I said.

It came out as a mumble. "Jeremiah Mayhew."

From the other side of the room, Woody said, "Goddammit."

CHAPTER 20

The election of a black man as president saved the National Brotherhood and the white supremacist movement. Watchdog groups said interest in the groups skyrocketed, post-Obama. That was especially clear with the National Brotherhood, which had crumbled apart like dried-out Play-Doh after the death of Dr. Carl Mayhew.

The National Brotherhood had been one of the first hate groups that embraced Internet technology, and they used it to play into white suburbanite fear. They revitalized their website, posting daily video screeds on the "impending race war" and the dangers of multiculturalism. They sold angry tomes, ranging from shitty teen romances that vilified race mixing, to Mayhew's own novel, "The Masters Chronicles," a bullshit fever dream advocating violent revolution. It became "The Catcher in the Rye" for the intolerant; three separate racially-motived spree killers cited it as inspiration in their massacres. The National Brotherhood sponsored a yearly musical festival on the compound, filled with proto-punk hate screamers with bad haircuts and simple lyrics that proclaimed white power. The organization restarted a music label it had during the Nineties. This time, alongside the punk and death metal, they signed a bunch of muttering white guys and called it "rap." Irony didn't seem something these guys appreciated fully.

Numbers for the Brotherhood grew, as they held rallies, went viral on social media, did whatever imaginable seemed necessary to become a viable presence, to make being a white supremacist palatable and something you could talk about with the neighbors at the HOA barbecue. What they failed at, though, was noticing how many of them looked like the adult versions of those kids who ate paste in school. You remember those kids. Did you want to associate with them then? Why the fuck would you want to associate with them now?

The game-changer for the Brotherhood, though, came with Monica Mayhew. The daughter of Dr. Carl Mayhew, Monica became the public face for the Brotherhood, a photogenic facade to push the group's platform into the public debate. The news shows loved her because she was attractive, with master's degrees in economics and art history. Well-dressed, well-spoken, easy on the eye, she excelled at selling the Brotherhood's message, which on the surface focused less about the perceived evil of Jews and blacks and Muslims and more about embracing "European culture" and "living within the cultural divide."

Pundits and politicians shifted the conversation and made it about "an illegitimate presidency, with a foreign-born Muslim in the White House," or "securing the borders to stop the influx of terrorists and disease," though, and Monica Mayhew stopped sounding crazy so much as just another voice claiming to speak for "the forgotten man, the disenfranchised, the sons and daughters of the first Americans." The world caught up with the white supremacist, it seemed.

There was a younger brother, too. Jeremiah Mayhew. Where Monica became a familiar face on TV, Jeremiah remained more mysterious, existing behind the scenes and away from the publicity. Word was how Carl Mayhew groomed Jeremiah early on to take over the reins of the National Brotherhood, to allow Monica to become its ambassador to the wider world. But no one had seen him in years. The skinny in government circles, the ones that monitored hate group activity, was that he was in hiding, maybe in the stages of planning an action that would bring the Brotherhood back to the forefront of the white power movement.

This is all what Woody told me after I'd taken Teller to his car and driven back to the farm. He had made calls to people. That's how he said it, too: "I called some folks."

"What folks?"

"Just folks. Folks who know things."

"Oh."

"And they said there's been a noticeable influx of cash into the organization, but nothing they can trace to anything illegal."

"What about the meth?"

"Irrelevant if no one will talk."

"I might have someone in mind."

"Think this person'll have anything to say."

"It never hurts to ask."

Browne's Hardware was eight aisles of product, with most items kept behind the counter. Bennett Browne was talking to another old man when I walked in, the bell over the door ringing as I came in.

"What about Sunday?" the old man said to Browne. "My grandson, he's wanting to go out, and we might on Sunday, if you wanna go with us."

Browne was barrel shaped, wearing a collared shirt and no-iron slacks and an apron with "Browne's Hardware" printed on it. He wore Coke bottle lenses and what little remained of his white hair tufted out around his head like cotton. He smiled at me. "Be with you in just a minute."

I nodded back and drifted down the paint aisle. The old man said goodbye and left and Browne was behind me.

"Whatcha thinking about painting?"

I didn't hear him, and I jumped a little. He laughed as I did a slow spin toward him.

"Sorry for scaring you," he said. "There anything in particular

I can help you with?"

I looked over the old man. He cast a curious look at me and raised his eyebrows.

I took a deep breath and said, "I'd love if you'd tell me why you're helping the Brotherhood cook meth."

The casual smile never left his face. "Well fuck-a-doodle-do," he said softly.

He flipped the sign to "Closed" on the entrance and we moved into the office in back.

The cork board behind his desk was covered with photos of a little girl, ranging from infancy to about six years ago. There were pictures of farm animals, of Santa and Jesus, of a little girl and a man fishing with the words "Me and Grampy" written over the figures, drawn in crayon or magic marker.

"My granddaughter's work," he said when he saw me looking at them. He took a seat behind the desk and I took the visitor's chair opposite him. "She lives in Pittsburgh with my son and his wife."

"See her much?"

"Not as much as I want to. I can't imagine there's a grandparent alive who says they see too much of their grandkids. They say grandkids are your reward for not killing your own children." He said it with a laugh meant to bury to discomfort of the situation. There wasn't enough heavy equipment to bury this shit.

The part of being a cop I had always hated was asking the painful questions. I opted to plunge in head first. "How'd this start, Mr. Browne?"

He tapped his fingers across his desktop. "About a year ago, I got this call from Denny Fitzgerald, who owns Fitz's Pharmacy."

I had memories of Fitz's from my childhood. I remembered picking up prescriptions there as a kid with Billy. We'd get lunch at the counter. Tuna salad and milkshakes. Don't judge; it had seemed like a good idea when I was eight.

"Anyway, he told me that someone from the Brotherhood had come to him, told him he wanted to buy boxes of Sudafed from him, off the books. Not just boxes, but whole cases. Denny, he's not stupid. No one's buying cases of Sudafed because they've got allergies. Denny asked me what I thought he should do, and I told him he should go talk the sheriff, make him aware of the situation. I'd no sooner got off the phone with him when a man walked into the store and told me he wanted to talk."

"What'd he look like?"

"Regular looking guy. Beard. Dark hair. On the youngish side of things."

Jeremiah Mayhew. "Go on," I said.

"He handed me a list, told me these were things he's to send people to buy. And I saw what he was buying, and it was ingredients for a meth lab."

"This is when you called Sheriff Simms, right?"

Browne picked up a plastic photo cube from his desk. Each side was a different photo of his granddaughter. He turned it around and around in his hands. "He had photos of Emily. They were at the zoo up there in Pittsburgh. Denny told me later they mentioned his wife. She's in a nursing home in Fairmont. Alzheimer's. She doesn't even know who he is anymore." He replaced the cube on his desk. "Found out this young guy was hitting another pharmacy in town, Wilson's, and more hardware stores. We're local, so people tell themselves no one notices what we're buying."

"Has anyone noticed?"

"Not yet. Guess we're like the pharmacies you hear about where they've sell enough painkillers to give a dozen bottles to every man, woman, and child there. People don't pay attention to little town, even if they do, what are we going to say? Guys like Denny and me are at the end of the race. We talk to the police, and what happens to the people we love? I don't want to go into the grave knowing my granddaughter was hurt because

I tried to do the right thing?" Browne shrugged. "I woke up one day and realized I'd invested an entire life in one place, and that no one will care when I'm not here anymore. That's everywhere you look in Serenity; there's not the town that used to be here. When it's all said and done, you think anyone'll notice Serenity's locked the doors and turned off the lights for the last time? No one sees anything they don't want to see, Mr. Malone." He stood and stretched. Joints popped and cracked. "I'm seventy-three years old. I'm not the picture of who you expect to be involved in a drug ring, am I?"

"I don't suppose you are, Mr. Browne."

"Who's your family? Who's your dad?"

"Billy Malone. He worked for Montgomery Mining and Energy."

Browne nodded. "I know him. Don't see him much."

"He keeps to himself."

Browne walked toward the office door and we headed back into the store. "I remember your mother." His voice dropped to a notch above a whisper. "She was a good woman. Shame what happened."

"Thanks," I said. I'd get that from old folks, people who remembered my mother's death. Nothing I could say there but "thank you."

We stood at the store entrance. Sodium vapor lights hummed outside. It was after six, and the streets were rolled up in Serenity. The bars were open, but businesses has moved to the big box stores outside of town now. Sidewalks were empty.

"Where's this put us, Henry?" Browne said. "What's next?"

"I guess next I'll go home and make hamburgers and feed my dog."

He motioned between us with his forefinger. "What about this? What we discussed tonight?"

I set the flat of my hand on the door, ready to push it open. "I don't know what you're talking about, Mr. Browne. I came in looking for paint."

CHAPTER 21

"What the hell, Henry?" Jackie said. "What the hell?"

We were at the hot dog stand in Serenity, having lunch. Jackie plowed his way through a third hot dog with everything. I had a half-finished hot dog sitting in front of me.

I shared everything I'd discovered up to this point, excluding stuff about Browne, because I couldn't think of a reason for the police to bust the old man. A week into all this, and I was already making moral judgments. Woot for me.

Jackie unwrapped the foil surrounding a fourth hot dog.

"Aren't you on a diet?" I said.

"Screw that. I'm stressed out. I'm a stress eater."

"How much stress does one person have?"

"Back off. You're already a goddamned boil on my dick as is."

"I'm offering you an open door to take down the National Brotherhood."

"I need the 411 on that cook house so we can shut it down."

"It won't close the operation. The best it'll do is stop it for a while. They'll just figure out somewhere new to make product."

"You have a better idea then?"

"Richard Walters and the fucking National Brotherhood, Jackie. It's so obvious. They're the lynchpin in this entire thing. You go after them, you shut down a massive drug shop, take out a scummy group of white power skinheads, and make your career in the meanwhile."

Jackie took a bite of hot dog. "I've already got a career, and it doesn't involve a partner in a massive state-wide law firm and trusting the word of a dipshit who joined a group of fellow dipshits just because they were all the same color as him. Besides, there's been folks going after the Brotherhood for years, and nothing happens. You'd think evolution would take hold, and they'd go extinct, or they'd dry up and blow away like an old dog turd, but they keep going and going, being another thing that makes us look like morons."

A quarter-sized drop of slaw and chili splattered across the front of his shirt. He flung the hot dog down and tried to wipe the mess off with a napkin, and he just made it worse, smearing it deep into the fabric. He crumpled the napkin into a ball and threw it next to the hot dog.

"Goddammit!" he said. Then quieter, again, "Goddammit." He huffed out a little breath of air. "Livvie's gonna be all over my ass about this shit. Stays on my ass, saying I come home wearing more than I eat." A thin smile appeared. "She's got no idea how much I can eat."

"I'm gonna bet she does." I ate some chips. "There's a lot going on here, Jackie. The meth house, that's low-hanging fruit. Walters and the Brotherhood, that's the heart of all of this."

"Any chance you're saying that because you got bitch-smacked by those two white-trash crackers?"

"Listen, I've spent the past two years in Serenity minding my own business, and as soon as I poke around Richard Walters, I got my ass handed to me, so pardon me if that put me in a foul humor. But one of them even bothered to confess that he got told to come smack me around, with Jeremiah Mayhew."

"None of that shit you're telling me would ever last thirty seconds in a courtroom after a judge finds out you and your friend went Guantanamo on that kid."

"Which is why you need to come in and get Richard Walters and beat him with a phone book—"

"'Beat him with a phone book'? The actual living fuck, Henry.

How do you think we do things around here?"

"I don't care how you handle it so long as Walters admits he killed Bobbi Fisher, or had her killed, and he's involved with the National Brotherhood. That opens the door to take down the meth operation. The fucking point is you're looking at the cook house, and that's nothing but some shiny thing to distract you from the real prizes here."

"We can't be for sure Bobbi Fisher is dead. There's no corpse. We've got nothing that says she's dead."

"Don't be fucking naive, Jackie. We both know she's dead."

Jackie sighed and wrapped the remains of his lunch in the foil, shoved himself off of the stool and dumped everything into a garbage can. I followed him outside. The wind picked up, and the bitter freeze cut through me until my bones ached. I was still healing from the beat down, not as quickly as I would have liked.

We walked in silence back to Jackie's state police cruiser. He leaned against the car's trunk. "Let this go. This isn't me asking, either. This is a straight-up order. The Bobbi Fisher thing was supposed to get your head out of your ass and your ass out of the trailer, but it's moved into a thing well past your paygrade. I'm telling you to walk away from this now. If Bobbi's attached to this somehow, it'll come out, don't worry. But until then, this can't be your worry."

Jackie was right. The asshole. I had no business keeping my nose in this anymore. It was more than Bobbi Fisher. I should step back and let the professionals handle it.

"You're going after the meth house, aren't you?" I said. "Everything else here, and it's just the cooks you're worried about."

"It's more than that, and you know it. It's dominoes. You gotta knock down the first one to take down the rest."

"And what about Richard Walters?"

"What about him? What do we have so far? Conjecture. There's nothing that says he had anything to do with Bobbi

Fisher, whatever happened to her."

"Tell me it's not because of that law firm."

Jackie didn't say anything. He didn't have to. It gurgled away in the bottom of my gut.

Fuck. That. Shit.

I caught Jackie trying to not look at me. Wait a minute. Was that pity in those eyes? Oh fuck you, asshole. Don't you fucking feel sorry for me. I'll smack you down like the borderline-Type 2 bitch you know yourself to be.

"Fine," I said. "You boys have at. Have a great time with it." I pulled up the collar on my coat. "I didn't give a shit about this anyway."

"You're lying," Jackie said. "That's your problem, Henry, is you do fucking care, and you want to behave like you don't."

"Yeah, well, you're fat," I said. Oh how clever.

Jackie called out my name as I walked away. "Go home, Henry! Don't do anything stupid! You hear me? Henry? HENRY! GO HOME!"

I rounded the corner and found a bar midway down the street. Not much crowd this early in the afternoon. It was safe and warm and anonymous. I ordered a shot, downed it, and ordered another.

And another. And another. And another.

Boom, boom, boom, boom.

I don't remember much that came next.

This is what I heard happened afterward:

• The state police brought in Teller, who told them he didn't know anything. They grilled him for hours and got nothing for the effort and had to let him go.

• The state police and the sheriff's department found the cook house, an old double-wide on a hillside with its own generator and four cooks working twelve-hour shifts. The cooks stated they were working independently, and had been robbing local businesses for supplies. No one said anything about the Brotherhood.

• Browne's body was found in his house three days later. The medical examiner determined he had fallen down his stairs and broken his neck.

• The police questioned Walters in Bobbi Fisher's disappearance, then released.

Christmas came and left. I don't remember much of it. Any of it, if I'm truthful here. I don't remember Doria calling me. I don't remember her leaving voice mails. I don't remember Billy coming by to make sure I was alive. I don't remember the times I must have driven to the convenience store, blasted out of my mind, to buy more beer. I don't remember Woody pounding on my door. I didn't have to hear that Dan Fogelberg song again.

I don't remember it becoming the new year. That's three weeks of my life. Completely gone. Three weeks I'll never get back.

I start remembering things around the time Bobbi Fisher showed up at my front door.

CHAPTER 22

It was a little after ten on a Tuesday morning and Pabst Blue Ribbon sounded good for breakfast when someone knocked at my door.

"Fuck off!" I yelled. It was likely Billy since I'd run off any other soul who might give a good goddamn about whether I drowned in a pool of my own vomit. If it was Billy, about now would be when he'd yell something parental—in the school of "Suck my cock, you ungrateful pile of shit!"—and storm back to his house. By knowing I could speak, and therefore was alive at least in the biological sense, if not the philosophical meaning, he could feel he'd done his fatherly duty, and I didn't want to deny the old man that.

The knocking continued, though. "I said, 'fuck off!'" I threw extra emphasis into my voice. There was more pounding at the door. I cursed and pushed myself up off the couch, tried to steady myself and failed, and tumbled forward, landing flat on my face.

Izzy gave me the hairy eyeball from her post next to the couch. She spent her days watching me—loads of intense dog staring. Her head moved in the arc of my collapsing body as I hit the floor. She walked over and sniffed me a few times and licked my face.

I didn't put up much resistance. Normally I would have, considering the places where her tongue often went. But if we're being truthful here, anywhere on Izzy was cleaner than anywhere on me right then, so I gave it a good "Oh, what the hell?" and let her keep going.

This asshole at my door, however, didn't give up. It took on a ferocity you expect when you owe money to people with "the" as a middle name.

"If I give you money, will you go away?" I said, and held my breath. Partially because a wave of nausea hit me and I wanted to vomit, and partially because if they took me up on the offer, I was fucked. Maintaining a constant bender isn't cheap, even when you buy from the bottom of the shelf.

A female voice said, "I'm looking for Henry Malone."

I didn't recognize the voice. It couldn't be Doria. I accessed a vague memory of talking to her, and of her asking me what was going on, but there wasn't much besides that. I didn't count on her making a return appearance to Chez Malone anytime soon.

"He's dead," I said, timing my words between slurps from Izzy's surfboard-sized tongue.

"Really?"

"Yep." I swatted at Izzy to stop. She got a few more licks in, then hauled herself back to her spot. I pushed myself onto my knees. It hurt like the proverbial motherfucker. "Leave a message, and I'll pass it on to him."

A pause, and then, "How you gonna do that if he's dead?" She sounded confused.

I scooted over to the couch, took a firm hold on the arm, and worked my way to my feet.

"Ouija Board." I pressed hard on the couch arm. My legs wobbled. I wasn't sober, but I was somewhere close enough to be casing the neighborhood. I needed a drink. "If you've got anything you wanna say to Elvis, I'll give that a run, too."

The pause that followed was long enough to fool me into believing she had left.

"Mr. Malone?"

Like most things in life, I was wrong.

I clutched the wall as I shuffled out of the living room and toward the front door. I caught hold of the doorknob as my balance gave way and opened the door.

She looked different from the pictures. She'd dyed her hair red, and it was all stuffed underneath a Cincinnati Bengals baseball cap. She'd lost weight and had dark rings underneath her eyes. She swam under the bulk of a heavy winter coat. But there was no mistaking who she was.

"Mr. Malone," she said. "I'm Bobbi Fisher. People tell me you've been looking for me."

I put on coffee, locked the bathroom door, and puked for a few minutes. When that ordeal finished, I took a shower hot enough to wipe off the first two layers of skin. I avoided looking in the mirror as I dried off. I wouldn't like what would be looking back at me.

I dressed in the cleanest jeans and T-shirt I had and found Bobbi at the kitchen table, sipping coffee and petting Izzy. Izzy had plopped her head on Bobbi's knee, resting on its side, moving around as to give Bobbi's fingers the best access to the places in dire need of a scratching.

I poured myself a cup and sat down across from Bobbi. She took a pack of cigarettes from her coat pocket. "Mind if I smoke?" she said. I told her I didn't mind so long as she gave me one. She was pretty when she smiled. Not a beauty queen, but in an honest, unpretentious way. I set a cereal bowl between us to use as an ashtray.

"How long have you been back?" I said.

"Since last night. Mitch and the girls didn't expect it, and the look on their faces when I showed up, you'd have thought they watched me crawl out of a grave."

"Not an unjustified response. There's a county full of people expecting to find you in a state of decomposition somewhere, Ms. Fisher. You mind telling me what happened?"

She knocked ash into the bowl. "Me leaving was shitty, Mr.

Malone, but I did what I had to do for my babies."

"Three months. You left three months ago, with your brother and his wife to raise your babies. Honey, you've lost any shot you had to get a 'Best Mom Ever' coffee mug next Christmas."

Her eyes met mine. "I've been crashing in someone's basement for those three months, and every night I've cried myself to sleep thinking about my girls, so don't act like you got any right to be a prick to me because you spent a little time asking questions about where I was."

"Then answer this question for me: What happened?"

She sucked down the last of her cigarette and lit a fresh one off of its dying embers. "I suppose you know I was fucking Richard Walters."

"Everyone seemed to know it but the police, and I'm sure they know now."

She shook her head. "The asshole." She blew tendrils of smoke out of her nostrils. "I worked at McGinley and Kurt because I had some secretarial classes over at the community college, though they're not 'secretarial' classes now; it's called being an 'administrative assistant,' which is funny since it's still filing papers and getting coffee and getting your ass smacked by the boss." She drank coffee. "I guess Richie—that's what he said everyone called him—he made it clear he was after me, and I kept saying, 'no,' and he kept wearing me down, and 'no' turned into 'yes.' It worked for a while. We liked each other."

She helped herself to another cup of coffee. "I was at his house about a week before everything, and we were just got done fucking. He's got this thing, he likes fucking in their bed, where he and his wife slept, that it's a turn-on for him. Anyway, the doorbell rang, and he freaked out because it was Tuesday and we'd told everyone we'd be in Marlington for a deposition. I thought it might be his wife but then again it's her house, so she wouldn't have much count to ring her own doorbell, would she?

"He looked out the window and said 'fuck' over and over. Told me to stay put. I'm naked, laying in another woman's bed,

I'm not sure where the hell it is he thinks I'll go, so I watch while he throws on pants and a shirt and answers the door.

"I could hear 'em talking at the doorway, and Richie said he's told them to not come to his house. Then one guy told Richie that he's not the boss of this deal, that this is the Brotherhood's operation, and people aren't not happy with the way the buys are coming.

"I got up and cracked the door and looked and there were two guys there. Richie looked real nervous, pacing around, and the skinny guy, he was smiling, and the other guy, he seemed very serious. Richie told them everything was fine, for them to focus on the product and the money, and how he would take care of the rest. They walked outside, and I looked out the bedroom window and watched them get into a car. The serious guy, he unlocked the driver's side door, stopped and looked up toward the house and he saw me in the window." Her body shook, as if fighting off a chill. "He had a look like he saw right through me. Like me being there mattered no more than a cat in an alleyway. Then they got in their car and started up and drove off.

"The next day, I took the girls to school, and he was parked across the street, smoking a cigarette. He was there when I picked 'em up at the end of the day, and he was there the next morning. When I came out of Kroger from buying groceries, Mr. Malone. It scared the fuck out of me."

"So you opted to bail and leave your girls here?"

Bobbi lit a new cigarette. "You think I'm stupid, or I'm a bad mother, but those girls are everything to me. I could have taken them and left, but I couldn't do anything to protect them. I've got a gun, but there's a world of difference between protecting me and protecting them. My brother, he was in the Army, over there the first time we invaded Iraq, and he's got nothing against killing someone, especially if it means keeping the girls safe. I called friends in Cincinnati, and they let me stay with them while I tried to figure things out. The girls were safer here, with my brother, than anywhere they'd be with me."

"So why d'you come back?"

She exhaled a cloud of smoke, seemed to contemplate it. "Missed my girls. And realized that being scared of dying ain't no way to live. First thing I did was see my brother and the girls, and he told me about you, so here I am."

"You let anyone else know you're back in town?"

"No one but my family."

"Then I need you to make sure they don't tell anyone. Don't call the police, talk to the neighbors, nothing."

"Why?"

"Because we need you to stay vanished a little while longer."

CHAPTER 23

Woody didn't say anything as I walked into the noon AA meeting. He stood at the other side of the room, chatting up with a few of the regulars. He saw me and he gave me a nod, but he kept on talking to the other guys while I poured a cup of coffee.

The meeting was a few folks bitching about the circumstances of their existence and the others grateful for whatever they had going on. When my turn rolled around, I passed. Woody gave the standard "Thanks, Henry," and moved on to the next drunk in line.

Everyone gathered outside to smoke after the meeting. Woody had his back against the stone, staring out at the parking lot.

"Bum a smoke?" I said.

Woody handed me the pack and matches. Once I had my cigarette lit, and he'd deposited everything back to their proper places, he said, "How you doing?"

"I'm sober today."

"It is one day at a time. I see you're choosing to rejoin the world?"

"Things came up."

"Must have been a hell of a lot of things. It's been a couple of weeks since I heard hide or hair of you. Plenty of shit going down in that time."

"I don't suppose you got your Christmas card."

Woody took a pull from the cigarette and dropped the butt to the ground and crushed it out. "I think you need to find a new sponsor, Henry. I'm not sure you want this, or you don't want it how I can help you."

"That's not it, Woody. It's—"

"No, that is it. That, and you're an arrogant prick, and an asshole, and you got shot and left the state police because you couldn't be 'Super Cop' anymore, and whatever else you tell yourself has wronged you in your life. Your mom, Maggie, all the other shit, that's the motherfucking past, Henry, and you need to treat it as such. You need to look at your goddamn here and now rather than—"

I leaned in close to him. "Bobbi Fisher is alive."

Woody stopped in mid-rant. He lifted his thick eyebrows into an expression that would have been surprise on most people, but on Woody, it instead registered as a mild interest.

"She showed up at my doorstep this morning," I said. "Right out of nowhere."

"Nothing on the news about her being back."

"Because no one knows."

"How is she?"

"She's fine, but she's got an interesting story to tell about Walters and the Brotherhood, and it's something we can use to make things connect."

"And now you need help."

"A smidge."

"A smidge of that help would come from me?"

"A smidge of that smidge would indeed come from you."

"It suspect there will be several smidges involved in this."

"There are multiple smidges."

Woody lit a fresh cigarette. "Where's she at now?"

"Billy's house."

"That's a serious fucking smidge right there."

"Billy's someone I trust to keep her safe."

"He might be the only person I know better armed than me."

"He doesn't carry canister grenades."

"I can hook him up if he's so inclined." He crossed his arms over his chest. "You gotta tell me you will not bail again. This shit, if you can't handle it, you need to let someone know who can."

"I've got this. But I can't do it myself, and I got big enough balls to say so, so I'm asking for help, which is why I'm asking if you want to go talk to the woman we have to keep safe from meth-cooking white supremacists?"

Woody smiled. "When you put it that way, the day gets a lot more interesting."

Billy had a shotgun resting on the dining room table and was reading the newspaper when Woody and I walked in. Bobbi was across from him, eating a sandwich and barbecue chips.

I introduced Woody to Bobbi. "You'll stay at Woody's while we figure out things with the Brotherhood," I said.

Bobbi gave Woody the up-and-down and took a drink of Mountain Dew. "This hippie's place is safe?"

"The farm's secluded," I said, "and he's got dogs and guns."

"Is that supposed to make me feel better?"

"Yes," Woody said. "That's the purpose of mentioning the dogs and the guns."

Bobbi ate another chip and excused herself to the bathroom.

Billy put down his newspaper. "What you boys getting yourself into?"

"Just a little sniffing around," I said. "Nothing to worry about."

Billy took a comb from his pocket and ran it through his hair as he talked. "The Brotherhood, they the ones who beat you up, uglied you up worse than life already had done?"

I looked at Woody. "You hear this? Imagine what it was like when I was twelve and chubby."

Billy shoved the comb back in his pocket and picked his

newspaper back up. "Never liked those assholes. Never knew no reason they had to go around, calling people niggers and beating up Jews and whatnot."

"You using the n-word sort of makes you sound like one of them," I said.

Billy gave the newspaper a good shake. "I'm an old man, so I can say what I want. It's a word, same as any other, and it's only worth whatever you think it's worth. I got no issue with no one, don't care what color they are, so long as they ain't got no issue with me." He glanced over to Woody. "You planning on helping this idiot do whatever the hell it is he thinks he's gonna do."

Woody smiled. "He'll need some help."

Billy gave his head a slow, mournful shake. "You're both retarded. You can't fight ignorance like that, not when it's stirred in with meanness, and all of 'em, that's what they've got, is stupidity mixed up with anger and fear. All they're looking for is folks to blame for why their lives are the shit storms they are, instead of looking at themselves."

I gestured down the hallway, toward the bathroom. "She's got kids. Someone's gotta do something or she'll just spend the rest of her life looking over her shoulder, being scared."

"We're all scared, son," Billy said. "It's choosing what to do with the being scared that makes you whatever you are."

CHAPTER 24

Doria opened her front door, looked at me, then slammed the door shut.

Success.

I rang the doorbell.

"I own a gun, Henry," she said from the other side of the door. "Guns. Multiple. I'll use 'em. All of them."

"That seems excessive."

"You don't fuck with women in menopause; we'll run over you and blame it on soy supplements."

"I need to talk. It's cold out here, and my knee isn't for shit, so it's gonna be hard for me to get down there to beg and be able to get back up. You wouldn't put a cripple through that, would you?"

The door cracked open enough to show one eye and a sliver of Doria's face. "Did you just call yourself a cripple?"

"Do I strike you as a man washed over with shame?"

"None whatsoever."

"Then can we move past that part of things and get to the part where I come inside and explain myself and I throw myself at your feet and beg forgiveness?"

The door opened wider. Full face. She wore a hooded sweat-shirt and sweatpants. She made sweatpants look hot, goddammit.

"I like the part about begging for forgiveness. You can start with that."

I held the door frame and lowered myself down onto my knees. I regretted it as soon I was down there, but if I'd learned nothing from my poker-playing adolescence, you sometimes had to go all-in.

I clasped my hands together and tried to resemble Oliver Twist. "Please, please, oh holy mother of God, forgive me for my sins and trespasses. For the wrongs I've committed, for the misdeeds of my wanton lifestyle. Can you see it in your heart to find pity on me, a poor, wretched worm of a man—"

The door swung open, and she reached out one hand. "For the love of Pete, get in here before the neighbors talk more than they do already."

We sat in the living room and drank coffee as I told her what had happened. She nodded without speaking and sipped from her cup. When I was done talking, I set my cup on the end table next to me and she rested her cup on the table close to her. She slapped me, picked her coffee back up, and took a drink.

"I wanted to get that out of the way now," she said. "Because you're an asshole."

I rubbed my face. Once the shock wore off, heat and sting rose to the surface. "A lot of people would back you up on that."

"Those people would be right. You need something," she said. "From me, I mean. You didn't show up only to grovel."

"Walters must be involved in the Brotherhood's meth operation, and I think he's using resources at the firm for it. What I need is someone with access to McGinley and Kurt case files. Someone who can see what Walters is working on, what he's been up to in the course of the past year, things can help tie him in with the Brotherhood."

"This person you're talking about, you know you're asking a lot of her, right?"

"I don't recall getting gender-specific with the pronouns, but I'd appreciate it, and so would Bobbi Fisher."

Doria's eyes went slit-thin. The same with her lips. "Know it's getting done for Bobbi, and it sure as fuck isn't getting done for you." She folded her hands in her lap. I'd never seen "forlorn" as an expression until that moment. "I was starting to care about you, Henry. I don't do that shit lightly."

"I don't have an excuse, Doria. I'm sorry."

Her face betrayed emotion, all of it hurting and pain. "Weeks passed by. Holidays passed by, and a year started, and you checked out of the world. Are you so selfish, something didn't go your way, you turn your back on everyone?"

She turned away from me. I reached for her hand. She drew back. Shook her head.

"Call me tomorrow." Her voice was thick and cracked. "On my cell phone. Don't call me on the office line." She swallowed a sob. "I need you to go now."

She didn't show me the way to the door. It was fine since I remembered the way out.

CHAPTER 25

Not long after the world discovered Y2K wouldn't turn everything into an apocalyptic wasteland, the West Virginia Legislature passed a bill that outlawed pre-existing video poker machines. Back then, the things were everywhere; you'd go to pay for a tank of gas at the holler convenience store, and there would be your neighbor Bubba, playing video poker between scratching off lottery tickets. I called it "the Appalachian retirement plan."

What the legislature did was to allow new machines to be set up in so-called "adult environments," which ended up being video poker parlors. These fucking things sprung up everywhere, and they all had cute names like "Emma's" and "Charlotte's". They usually sell food—chewy pasta served with canned sauce—and booze—box wine in a paper cup—but the focus is always on the five video poker machines the joint can have.

I was on my way home when I spotted Earl Teller's car in the parking lot of a place called Becky's. I pulled in and went inside.

Porn theaters have more ambience than places like Becky's. The five machines were lined up against the wall across from the entrance, and all five were busy when I walked in. An old guy with a walker played an end machine while middle-aged women worked the rest. One lady in the middle was snapping green beans into a pot as she picked cards on the touch screen. Country music played; it was something about the singer missing the girl he'd done wrong in high school. George Jones must have been spinning in his grave.

There were a pair of pool tables in the middle of the room, and Teller was shooting at one as I ordered a cup of coffee from the lady behind the counter. She filled a Styrofoam cup from a coffee maker and said, "Four bucks."

The words caught me as I was pulling cash from my wallet. I must have shown it on my face.

"Free refills," she said with a practiced lack of giving a shit. "Don't like it, go to Starbucks."

I handed her four singles, and she pointed me toward the creamer and sugar on the other side of the room. The creamer sounded chunky when I shook the container, and the only sweetener was packets of the pink stuff that caused cancer in lab rats. The coffee itself was lukewarm and old enough to see R-rated films without an adult. I tossed it into a garbage can and walked to the pool tables and took a cue from the rack on the wall, leaning against Teller's table.

"Let's play," I said.

Teller aimed up his final shot on the table, the nine ball into a side pocket. The cue ball tapped with the gentleness of young love and sent it into the darkness.

"I'm done for the night." He broke his cue down and placed it in a carrying case. "I got places to be, if it's all the same to you."

I fished quarters from my pocket and fed them into the coin slots. The balls clattered free and I racked them into the triangle.

"I can appreciate a young man such as yourself, what pressing social engagements you must have." I walked around and aimed up the break. "But understand that I'll be wherever it is you eat, sleep, shit, breathe, and, in the greatest of unlikelihoods, fuck. Get used to seeing my visage in your life, because you won't be able to pinch a loaf without knowing I'm close by. Also, because I know you're curious, 'visage' means 'face.'"

Teller threw his head back. "And what makes you think me and my brothers won't just come by, maybe do a little worse to you than we did before?"

"Because you come at me again, and my friend who water boarded you will take it next level, and once he's done with you, you'll wish you'd killed me, because I'll take you off at the knees with a chain saw. Playtime will be done, and you'll start finding chunks of yourself in your own goddamn stool." I readied my shot. "We playing or what?"

Teller seemed to think about it for a while, because I could smell smoke, or tires burning, or something. He set his carrying case down and took one of the coffee shop's cues from the wall.

"What we playing for?" he said.

"Whatever I wanna know. You good with that?"

"And what happens when I win?"

"I walk into the sunset, never to darken your doorway again. Sound fair to you?"

He rested the cue behind his neck and hung his arms off the ends, like he was on the cross. "Let's do this shit, fucker."

I kicked his ass.

I won't say it was without effort. Teller was good. This was probably the one skill he possessed. But I took him down in three games straight. It was beautiful to see, and it brought me far greater joy than it should have. He got more frustrated as the games progressed, and his shots got sloppier, and I cleaned the table off quicker each time. I never mentioned how I was my academy class's billiards champion, and in later years I made drinking money in Morgantown hustling tables from asshole law students.

When we finished, he looked like a kid who found out he wasn't getting a puppy for Christmas.

"Let me leave, wait a few minutes, and then you go," I said. "I don't want anyone to think anything undue about our relationship."

"Stop making it sound like we're faggots, you faggot."

Once I was outside, I had a smoke. He followed behind me

two minutes later.

"You call anyone in there?" I said. "You better not have, because I don't want to see headlights zooming up from the distance, and a cadre of your cracker-ass brethren trying to swoop in and kick my ass."

"No, I didn't call no one." He lit a cigarette. "That day, you and that other asshole, that shit wasn't fair. It was two against one."

"Same odds when you and Jeremiah Mayhew came by house."

He exhaled smoke. "I was just doing what I got told to do."

"A good little soldier." I unlocked the Aztek doors. "Get in. And put out that cigarette; no one smokes in my ride."

"Your ride's a piece of shit."

"It is, but it's my smoke-free piece of shit."

Teller looked at the cigarette. "I just fucking lit it."

"Then you can just fucking put it out."

He took a drag. "Know what I think is gonna happen? I'm gonna smoke this, I'm gonna tell you a 'fuck you very much,' and I'm gonna go get in my car and leave. Because you and me both know, you ain't gonna come running after me."

I scratched at the back of my neck. "Agreed. So what'll happen then is that I'm going to live on your ass like a painful little zit. I'll bear down on you until either you break, or you do something stupid and the Brotherhood beats you down. The funny thing with all this is, while you're no doubt stupid as hell, I gotta say I'm not sure you're as committed to the cause as you like to act."

He bared his teeth. They weren't good teeth, and it didn't make him look like a tough guy as much as a warning to children for better dental care.

"Never accuse me of betraying my race," he said.

"Implied nothing of the sort. I will say at my house, while your friend was working to put a hurt on me, you tried, in the whitest way possible, to get a groove going to Kanye, and that can't be something tolerated within your hateful little sewing circle."

Again with Teller and the thinking. It almost broke my heart to watch. You could tell all of those muscles had long since atrophied—not that he would have known what "atrophied" meant.

He crushed the cigarette into the ground and, without a word, walked around to the other side of the Aztek and got in.

CHAPTER 26

We found a holler, and I drove until we were past houses and paved roads and there was nothing but the full moon hanging high in the sky. I left the engine running and the heater chugging away.

"You're going to tell me what the Brotherhood's doing," I said.

Teller shook his head. "I picked up supplies. That's it. No one never told me anything."

"Who's selling for you?"

"What part of 'they don't tell me shit' are you not understanding?"

"Then what about where this money is going then?"

"I don't even do the pickups anymore. They sure as fuck never told me what they're doing with the money."

"Who does the money pickups?"

"No idea."

"What about the cookhouse? There's no way they quit after the bust, so where are they cooking now?"

"How many more questions you want to ask me, and me give you the same answer?"

"I'll keep asking until you tell me something useful."

Teller sighed. "You don't give a fuck, I get that, but The Brotherhood is all I've fucking got. A lot of that shit they preach at the compound, it's fucked up, I'll give you that. I don't take it all as gospel. Sure, I like Kanye and Drake and Biggie, and stuff we're not supposed to listen to, but I ain't the only one there into that shit, either. The Brotherhood, those people, they're it for me. My family's not worth a fuck. I've got no job. Didn't finish high school. Sure as hell not going to dig coal and maybe get myself killed. Only real anything I've got is the Brotherhood, and what you're doing is making me sell it out to you."

There was pain in his voice. Somewhere inside that reptilian brain of his, there was something looking for an explanation of right and wrong, and he was struggling to find the divide between the two.

"Listen, I don't get this thing with you all," I said. "And I don't care, either, so long as you don't hurt people, but the thing is, you are, and I can't be good with that, so I'm going to do what I can to make it stop."

He gave a little nod. "You were a cop, weren't you?"

"I was."

"Your friend, the one who hosed me down, was he a cop?"

"More like a force of nature."

"He's a fucking lunatic."

"He'd agree with you."

"You were nice, making him stop when you did, though. He would have kept on, wouldn't he?"

"Most likely. I don't think he cares for what you guys believe in."

"What do you think?"

"That life's too short to judge people on something like skin color, or what side of the border they were born on. You don't like someone, do it for a good reason, like if they drive with their turn signal on, or they go through self-checkouts with a full cart of groceries, or they like Adam Sandler movies."

Teller tapped his fingernails steadily against the window.

"You got any paper?" he said.

From the glove box I took an envelope from an unpaid parking ticket and a pencil. Teller wrote out a set of directions on the back of the envelope. His handwriting was terrible, the scrawl of a caffeine- and sugar-fortified eight-year-old. His hand trembled as he wrote. When he finished, he shoved everything toward me and stared out the window.

"Take me back to my car. I want to get away from you before you find some new way to fuck over whatever's left of my life."

I put the Aztek in gear, whipped it around, and drove back to Becky's. He kept his mouth shut the entire drive and slammed the door as he got out. His tires spun out gravel from the parking lot as he pulled out, roaring down the road into the night.

CHAPTER 27

Snow spit lazily from the sky, swirling back and forth across my windshield and scattering across the ground like confetti as I got to Woody's the next morning. It wouldn't stick, but it would remind you that it was still indeed winter, the season trying its damnedest to assert itself upon us, and doing so half-assed.

There was gunfire the closer I got to the house. Anywhere else, I would have worried, but this was Woody's, and gunfire almost counted as white noise there.

The roar of dogs barking threatened to blot out the sound of semi-automatic weaponry as I got out of the Aztek. About half of the pack came running toward me, encircling me, nipping at my feet. I followed the clatter of spent cartridges to the back of the house. Woody and Bobbi stood at the shooting range, Bobbi emptying the clip from an AR-15 into a target and Woody staring at his cell phone and holding a 9 mm pistol in my direction. When he saw me, he scanned the perimeter, dropped the gun to his side, and waited for Bobbi to finish shooting.

When she was done, she looked at Woody and smiled. She pulled her headphones off and he said something to her I couldn't hear, and she kissed him on the cheek and loaded a new clip into the weapon, opening fire again as he walked over to me. He took me by the arm and led me around to the side of the house.

Woody kept his eyes focused on Bobbi.

125

"I keep an eye this way, you keep an eye that way," he said.

"I can't see you then."

"That would be the idea."

"Makes it awkward to make fun of you."

"Again, kind of the idea."

I glanced toward Bobbi, then back at Woody. "Have you two—?"

"A gentleman never tells."

I laughed. "I guess she got over you being a hippie. What were you staring at on your phone while brandishing that weapon in my direction?"

"The security cameras around the house feed into an app on my phone, so I can check any of them from it. I watched you pull up and come around the house."

"You knew it was me and you still kept a gun pointed at me?"

"Check."

"Paranoia much?"

"Paranoia is another way of describing a complete awareness of your surroundings."

The gunfire stopped again.

"Woody!" Bobbi yelled.

"Right here," Woody said to her. "You wanna head on inside, give it a break?"

"Sure thing." She waved at me. "Hey, Henry!"

I made a half-turn to look at her, and Woody punched my shoulder. I pivoted my view back to the driveway. "Hey, Bobbi!"

"How's it going?"

"Good. We're getting shit done."

"Awesome. What are you staring at?"

"Nothing."

"Awesome," she said again. "I'll make tea."

"You do that," Woody said. "We'll be right on inside."

The screen door opened and shut.

"How's she doing?" I said.

"Pretty well," Woody said. "You can stop looking in that

direction now. Anyway, she misses her girls. She's a nice woman. Decent shot. We've been working on that, make her better than decent should the need arise."

"I'm hoping the need doesn't arise."

"As am I."

My cell phone rang.

Woody headed toward the back door and into the house.

I answered the phone. It was Doria.

"Hey there," I said, silver-tongued devil that I was. "How you doing?"

"I'm the queen of the universe, Henry. Do you wanna know why I called or not?"

So much for foreplay. "Sure. Fire away."

"Walters has been doing damn little, it seems, other than helping this company called Rockwell LLC file paperwork it needs to be street legal, and managing a series of electronic fund transfers to several international businesses."

"How international are we talking?"

"Generally in Mexico, though some cash is going to Eastern European countries. Places with 'stan' in their names."

"Any idea what Rockwell LLC is buying?"

"Doesn't really say. The paperwork is vague as fuck about details. There's a palpable odor of bullshit and the stench of a probable federal investigation if anyone got word of this."

"But there's nothing hinting at what they're buying?"

"I think I said that already, but I'll try to find another way of saying it so maybe you understand this time." Doria's voice turned tired. "The only reason I'm doing this is so Bobbi can have her life back. Otherwise, I'm regretting I ever met you."

"You're not the first person to tell me this, and I doubt you'll be the last, either."

"Hell of a legacy you're leaving in your wake. You always take a 'scorched earth' policy in relationships?"

"I don't leave memories; I only leave survivors."

"Fuck you, Henry. I do not need your tired-ass cynicism. I

have my life to deal with, with everything that goes with what the grown-ups do."

The words were swift, and I'll admit they hurt. I was sure that was the intent.

"I'll let you go then," I said.

"You already have," she said, and the line fell dead.

I found Woody and Bobbi inside at the kitchen table, drinking tea, Bobbi reading a handgun magazine and Woody working a Sudoku puzzle from the newspaper. Three dogs were sleeping on the floor.

Woody looked up from the puzzle. "How was your girlfriend?"

"Tread lightly there," I said. To Bobbi, I said, "This bastard treating you okay?"

"No complaints," she said. "The towels are a little scratchy, but he makes good crepes and—"

"Crepes?" I said. "You make crepes?"

Woody popped his neck. "Did she have anything useful to tell you, or she call to tell you to go to hell like a reasonable person would?"

"A little of both," I said. "Can we talk outside?"

Woody nodded, and we walked out on the front porch.

I pulled up the collar on my coat as a sharp wind blew across the porch. The snow was picking up though it wouldn't amount to much more than a dusting. The roads would remain safe, and children's dreams of a day off from school would be dashed.

I told him what Doria had told me. "I need to own up to being in over my head, Woody. When I started this, I thought it was about finding Bobbi, try to help her brother and her kids out—"

Woody shook his head. "That's not the truth and you know it. What it was about was you satiating something in your ego. About feeling like you had a purpose in life again, instead of being a gimp stuck in a trailer in Bumfuck, West Virginia, drinking himself to death and lying about it."

"You have a remarkably soft touch with people, Woody. You're not wrong, either. But it's blown up well beyond that, and now all I want is to make sure Bobbi stays alive, and that her daughters stay out of harm's way. Past that, this is becoming too much."

Woody cracked his knuckles. It was a huge noise, almost like fireworks, and it hurt me to hear it. "The Brotherhood's got the lab Teller told you about. I'll promise you it's not the only one. And obviously there's a lot more going on if Walters is moving all of that money around under bullshit excuses. That makes the issue at hand that the Brotherhood has real cash. Based on what you know about white supremacists, what are they likely to spend money on?"

"Guns and explosives?"

Woody nodded. "We need to make ourselves known to the Brotherhood. Stir their pot up, and give them a reason to sweat."

"The cook house would be a nice pot to stir."

"It would. You ain't had fun until you've blown up a meth lab."

"How many have you blown up?"

Woody opened the door to go back in. "Everyone's got to have a hobby, Henry."

CHAPTER 28

Calling what Woody and I had in mind a "plan" didn't quite do it justice. It was, at best, a scheme, some fragments of ideas we hoped would bond together and be enough to rile up the Brotherhood. Because it was, from the outset, unformed and half-assed, we decided using the cover of darkness that night might help it work, or at least keep us from getting killed.

There wasn't much left to do until then, though, and I was hungry, so I hit the Tudor's drive-through and drove home with the smell of a chili cheeseburger and fries filling my car with fumes of heart-clogging glory. That was when my cell phone rang.

The number showed up as an extension from McGinley and Kurt. Might be Doria. I hoped it was Doria. I didn't answer it immediately. I wanted to sound cool, somewhat detached, not eager and excited. I took a deep breath and answered the phone.

"Hello?" I said. My voice squeaked. I fucked up my attempt at being Steve McQueen in two syllables.

"Henry Malone?" It was a man's voice. Richard Walters.

"What the hell do you want, Walters?"

"We need to talk. Now." He slurred his words. Lunch was coming in liquid form that day.

"How much do you think we've got to say to one another?"

"Don't make this more of a goddamn chore than it is already. I'll be at O'Dell's Bar and Grill. Be there in twenty minutes."

O'Dell's was a sports bar down the street from the Parker

County courthouse, a place where attorneys would clear a bucket of beer while bitching about WVU's football team or the Pirates or the NBA finals blaring the background. The restaurant's half-dozen TVs were all tuned to different stations, most of them showing guys behind desks analyzing the activities of millionaires playing the games we used to play for free. Post-lunch, the crowd has thinned down to random customers trying to avoid the various inevitabilities of their lives.

Walters sat at the bar, hunched over a whiskey and soda. He had the haggard expression of a man living on little sleep. His hair was shaggier than when we'd met, flecked with more gray. From a distance you could tell he needed a shave and stronger deodorant. Closer, I saw his face was a patchwork of bruises fading from purple to blue. His eyes were puffy and swollen, and small cuts criss-crossed his cheeks and jawline. It all looked like work I was familiar with.

"Look rough around the edges, counselor," I said.

He stared across the counter and into the mirror on the wall. I waved at his reflection. He sipped his whiskey with a dearth of amusement.

"Buy you a drink?" he said.

"A Coke would be great."

"A Coke?"

"Pepsi if they don't have that."

He threw back the last of his drink in one swallow and motioned for the bartender. The bartender was chatting up a waitress who wanted to be anywhere other than where she was.

"Another one, Richie?" the bartender said. Richie. They must have shared a bond.

"Sure thing, and this wild man over here wants a Coke. Put it on my tab."

The bartender made Walters' drink, poured me a Coke, set them each on napkins in front of us, and returned to talking to the waitress. I bet they were dissecting pertinent social and political issues. Probably involving a Kardashian.

"You look like you got worked over there, counselor," I said. "You got problems?"

Walters took a drink of his whiskey and soda. His movements felt small and deliberate, and he winced in pain as he made them. "This is nothing. I'll deal with it. I got other fucking issues. I got shit-canned today. The rest of the partners decided I wasn't carrying my weight."

"Can't believe they let someone like you go without throwing you out a window first." I drank soda. "It's that easy to fire a partner in a law office?"

"There's always escape clauses in partner contracts. When there's a majority vote, they can dropkick you right out the door. It's a great big giant ass fucking without lube. They throw you out after twenty-two years. Fuck. Decent thing would be a reach around, but they bend you over and lay it to you."

"That's so much anal sex imagery, counselor." I finished my soda. "Freud would have a field day with that. Goddamn shame when a man figures out he's runs out of options, isn't it?"

"I get where you're going with that, so forgive me if I'm not about to let your shitty philosophy ruin my buzz."

"Then let's cut to the chase and you can explain what I've done to deserve the pleasure of your company. You may recall I'm the guy you sent goons after to knock around."

The bartender looked our way. Walters nodded, and the bartender refilled his drink and went back to the waitress. His moves on her so obvious Ray Charles would have noticed, and she smiled and swatted them down like King Kong with biplanes.

"That beating you took, I had nothing to do with that," he said. His head had dropped so low it threatened to be swallowed by his shoulders. "I can't say I blame 'em, and you deserve a good smackdown on the regular, but I didn't set anyone out on you."

I motioned for another Coke. I rattled the ice around the inside of the glass. A moment passed through my head where I thought how great it would be with whiskey in it. That moment passed.

"There wasn't any reason for them to come after me," I said. "They made sure to say for me to stay out of other people's business, and the timing made sense since yours was the only business I was getting into."

"Don't know what to tell you, Malone. Maybe they heard what an asshole you are, and this was like a 'welcome wagon,' except it was a 'stay the fuck away wagon.'" He laughed at that, then turned serious again. He had emotional shifts going on like tectonic plates. Alcohol wasn't the other thing in his system. "That bullshit at the motel, with you and the photos, that did me no favors. It was bad enough, the cops came calling right before Christmas, asking about Bobbi. My wife, she was asking me why the cops were asking me questions, and I had to tell her they were talking to everyone."

"You could have told her the truth. Been a nice change for you."

"You don't know my wife. Rachel's got the purest heart of any person I've ever met. She might not have believed me even if I told her everything."

"That why you married her? The idea she could redeem that crusted scab of a soul you got?"

He held up two fingers. "One: You're getting philosophical again, and I'm getting drunk, so fuck you." He pulled back the forefinger, leaving the middle riding high. "And second: Fuck you again."

I stood up. "Well, as pleasant as this has been, and trust me, it hasn't, I'm gonna go—"

He grabbed my wrist. His eyes filled with a mixture of fear and anger, mingled with desperation. Someone could have mistaken him for a human being if they hadn't known any better.

"Sit down," he said.

I pried his hand loose from me. He didn't give much resistance. "Why did you fucking call me, Walters?"

"I need you to find Bobbi for me. I've got cash; I can pay you."

"When I came calling earlier, you made it clear you didn't

give two shits about her. What's changed?"

"The Brotherhood's convinced she's got something of theirs, and they want it back."

"What could Bobbi have that the Brotherhood would want?"

He shook his head. "That's doesn't matter. Not even the motherfucking point. This thing…it's Bobbi. If you don't find her, they'll kill me, Malone."

"I'm waiting to hear the bad part of this."

"Jesus Christ, Malone. Have some goddamn humanity about you, at least."

"This thing you keep dancing around, is it why they beat you like a piñata?"

"Yeah. I kept telling 'em I didn't know what they were talking about, and they didn't believe me."

"They kept hitting you until they realized the story wouldn't change. You're lucky they stopped when they did."

"I'm well fucking aware, trust me. Had to tell Rachel that I got robbed leaving work. She bought that bullshit story, too. Wanted to call that sanctimonious prick of an ex-husband, the sheriff, and file a report."

"You told her you're part of the jobless rabble yet?"

"No, and I'm not going to. Not yet. Not until I figure this out." He looked at me again. "I need to find Bobbi, Malone."

"Then you'll tell me what's going on with you and the Brotherhood. That's what this will cost you, is you telling me the goddamn truth."

He sighed. "Fine." He finished his drink. "You fucking prick."

CHAPTER 29

"I was in Wheeling a year ago, working this insurance case for a construction company. There were liability issues—" Walters waved his hands around. "None of that's important. No, here's what's important. I'm in the hotel bar. I'm drinking and this blonde—" He smiled the smile of a man remembering something he shouldn't share but planned to, anyway. "She was hot as hell. Big tits. She sits down next to me, and starts drinking, and I'm a gentleman. I buy her a drink. We start talking. She's funny. She's smart. Her hand ends up on my knee, working its way up north. I do what any man would have done; I took her up to my room, and I fucked the living hell out of her. And she was something else, man. She should have had a height requirement to be that kind of ride."

"Ever the gentleman, Walters."

"The next morning, she's gone. Fine, because I'm hungover, and that's not when I like having to deal with crazy bitches. I call downstairs and have 'em bring me breakfast and a bloody Mary, to steady my stomach. When room service shows up, the guy brings in the newspaper and there's the blonde's picture on the front page, talking at a fucking neo-Nazi rally. Only they're not calling it 'neo-Nazi' or 'KKK,' anything like that. They're calling it 'European heritage.' But the blonde, the blonde is Monica Mayhew. You know who that is, right?"

"I'm aware you knocked boots with the queen of the neo-Nazi

135

movement, which makes you a fresh form of stupid, Walters."

He drank more of his whiskey and soda. "A week later, I got an email with a video file attached titled something like 'You Should Open Me.' It's video of me laying it to Mayhew. I'm plowing her like the back forty, man. And there's no disguising it's me. My face is there, big as life. It looks like cell phone video, where she set the goddamn thing up and let it roll, and I was drunk, and I didn't notice or care. I freak out. I'm a married man, a partner at a huge law firm. What do you think happens if shit like that got out?"

"You were all but bragging about you and Bobbi, so it's not like you're modest in your indiscretions."

"Not even the same fucking same. Bobbi was a white trash skank, and at a place like McGinley and Kurt, people expect you to bone the help. It's almost a perk of the job: good dental, vision, and blow jobs. Mayhew's completely different. She's on TV talking about white nationalism. You know the client base you get when you get associated with people like her? Toothless goons in flip flops and T-shirts about pro wrestling."

"Remind me when I'm supposed to feel sympathy for your situation."

"Let me finish my story, okay? So I get this phone call and it's Mayhew, and she says 'Tell me what you think about our little movie.' She had this sick little laugh, real satisfied with herself, and it was because she had me right by the balls, and all she needed to do was squeeze."

He finished his drink, and the bartender was there before Walters could say anything, replaced it, and disappeared again. He emptied half of the glass and looked at me. "What was I saying?"

"That Monica Mayhew said you had a little dick."

He snarled. "The goddamn cunt. She did. She fucking did." A confused look crossed his face. "Wait a minute. I didn't say that."

"The gist is that you got blackmailed into helping the Brother-hood."

He jabbed toward me with a wavering finger. "What you said. That. They told me I'd have to help them set up an LLC—"

"Rockwell, LLC."

"Right. How d'you know?"

"Magic 8 Ball. Keep talking."

"What they have me do is making these wire transfers and payments to companies."

"And you, the pathetic dipshit you are, aren't ever the least bit curious why they picked your narrow ass out of every legal rat and ambulance chaser in this state."

Walters shook his head, and drops of slobber shook loose from the corners of his mouth. He had more shimmy than a bowl of Jell-O on a waterbed during an earthquake. "I don't like your fucking attitude, Malone," he said. At least, that's what it sounded like. It also sounded like a string of consonants and vowels racked around the inside of his mouth like bingo numbers. "I called you 'cause I need your help. You don't get the shit I'm dealing with right now."

"So tell me. Educate me about your woes."

He held a finger up and swayed like he was battling a strong wind. "I will." He pushed himself upright and slid off the barstool to his feet. "But first, I'm gonna go piss."

As soon as the soles of his shoe touched the floor, Walters passed out and face-planted on the floor. Watching it was the best part of my day so far.

The bartender said this was Walters' norm, that he called a cab to get him home when it happened. I told him to not bother, and I walked Walters to my car and loaded him into the passenger seat.

His driver's license gave his address as a subdivision just outside of town, one of those sets of McMansions built during the real estate boom of Bush 2.0, when a pulse got you a mortgage.

Walters mumbled throughout the drive to his house, and

sometimes I understood a word or two he said. Once it sounded like "I love you, honey." I hoped it wasn't meant for me. I assumed it wasn't meant for his wife, either.

I pulled into the driveway and automatic exterior lights lit up the front like a prison yard. A fit woman in a Victoria's Secret T-shirt and yoga pants came out. She may have been five frenemies away from her own reality show, with big blonde hair and makeup layered like an onion. Underneath it all I bet there was an attractive woman, but it would have taken Indiana Jones to find her, and instead of trusting that, she had turned herself into the expectation of attractiveness. I guessed she was Rachel, Walters' wife, and Sheriff Simms' ex.

I negotiated Walters out of the car, threw one of his arms around my shoulder, and walked him to the front door. He was nothing but dead weight, slumped at the knees, dragging his feet along.

She smiled as we got closer. "Thank you so much for helping him get home." She took hold of him and steered him toward the front door.

I started to help her get him inside when she said she had him. This wasn't undiscovered country for her.

I was halfway back to the Aztek when she said, "Sir? Sir?"

Rachel Walters used one of her shoulder to pin her husband against the door and keep him upright. "Do I owe you anything?"

"Not a thing. Just glad he got home safe."

"So am I." She looked at Walters. There was genuine affection there. The fuck if I understood why.

I had the driver's side door open when she said, "You didn't tell me your name. Are you a friend of Richie's?"

I looked over the roof of the car to her. "No, ma'am. I'm sure as hell not his friend."

I got into my car and drove away.

CHAPTER 30

Woody met me at his door dressed in a black turtleneck and black cargo pants and black lace-up boots, looking like he was ready to set to free POWs with Chuck Norris.

"I need to talk to Bobbi," I said.

"What about?" A defensive expression crossed his face. Perhaps I should have waited until he was less well armed, which would have been never.

I told him about Walters. He led me into the living room. Bobbi was stretched out on the couch, reading a paperback.

"Hey, commandoes," she said, setting the book aside.

I looked at Woody. "You told her?"

"I'm not dressed to pick up a pizza," he said. "This involves her."

I shrugged. What-the-fuck-ever. To Bobbi, I said, "Walters is looking for you."

She sat upright, shifting straight from relaxed to worried, ignoring other emotional gears along the way. "Why?"

"I don't know," I said. "He passed out before he could tell me. But he admitted working with the National Brotherhood, and he said you have something they're looking for. What's he talking about?"

She shook her head. "No idea. All I did was what he asked me to do. I pushed paperwork, that was it."

I narrowed my eyes, tried to look intimidating. I probably

just looked stoned. "Are you sure that's it? Nothing else?"

She nodded. "Swear to God, Henry. You met Walters. You think that man would tell the truth about anything. I just want this done so my daughters and me can get back to whatever life we've got left."

Woody placed his hand on my shoulder. "Work for you?"

Not really, I thought, but we had to be for the time being.

"Sure," I said. "We're rock stars."

He smiled. "Then let's go have fun."

We pulled up the narrow road at a snail's pace, feeling each pothole and rut as we eased through, stopping and cutting the engine around a mile from the trailer. The address Teller had given me for the cook house was up a country road, away from utility lines and most of humanity, in a deserted chunk of the county. Woody and I wandered for an hour trying to find the road before we stumbled across it.

From the rear of the Aztek, Woody and I each took one-gallon cans of gasoline, a nine millimeter pistols, and a sawed-off 12-gauge pump-action shotgun, and headed off into the brush that lined the road. The growth was thick and thorny, heavy despite the winter. We kept eyes on the ground, checking for trip wires and IEDs.

I'd asked early on if we needed flashlights and got nixed by Woody like I'd offered to carve the roast beef at a PETA banquet.

"Unless you want to make us easier targets, we do this in the dark," he had said.

The trailer was a single-wide dropped onto a cleared-out section of land set well away from anything. It made my digs look luxurious, with the aluminum siding rusted and peeling to expose tattered insulation. Someone had tiered concrete blocks to makes steps inside. Light shone through the curtains in the windows. Jimi Hendrix played inside, but it was barely audible over the steady pumping of the genny that powered the place.

"That's 'Voodoo Chile,'" I said.

"Sounds like it," he said.

"You suppose they know he was black?"

"He was half-Native American, too, and even utter ignorance has to appreciate good music."

We rushed through the clearing, me to the left and Woody to the right. We crouched low and uncapped the gas cans once we were at the trailer and moved clockwise, pouring fuel on the ground. I held my breath—not because of the smell, but because I didn't want a random spark to ignite an explosion inside the trailer while I was holding a gasoline can. The resulting fireball would have been visible from space.

We finished and poked around the side to the front of the trailer, saw each other, gave a nod, and crept toward the door.

The goal was simple: Lure everyone out and set the meth lab on fire. This wouldn't be the Brotherhood's only lab, but something like this would get their attention. At best, it would cause enough chaos to force the Brotherhood into the open; at worst, they would do something stupid and give the police something to bust them on. If all else failed, at least it was one less meth lab in Parker County. Like I said, it wasn't much of a plan, but it was what we had.

We paused at the concrete block stairs. Woody gestured toward himself, then the door, then me. It looked cool and military. I nodded. He stood up and took a first step up as the door opened from the inside.

The skinhead coming out wore a heavy coat over a white T-shirt and blue jeans and cowboy boots. He had a cigarette hanging from his lips as he stood at the open door and stared back into the trailer.

"I don't give a fuck if he was Chief Sitting Fucking Bull, he was a goddamn nigger, and I'm not listening to that shit all night," he said, lighting the cigarette and taking a draw. "When I'm done with this, we're listening to some real music. Like Conway Twitty."

Woody looked straight up at the skinhead. The skinhead stared forward, smoking as he descended the steps. Once the skinhead had both feet on solid ground, Woody jumped to his feet and slammed the butt of the shotgun into the back of his head.

The skinhead dropped to his knees with a stunned guttural grunt. Woody pounded the shotgun into his face. The skinhead's nose shattered and blood spurted as he fell backwards. Woody hit him again, this time with his fist. Teeth shattered, and bones cracked in the skinhead's face. Woody was pulling back for another punch when I whispered, "Woody!" He stopped in mid-swing.

The skinhead's face was already purple and swollen. Blood poured out of the twisted bag of cartilage that had been his nose, crimson glugging down the sides of his skull and pooling around his ears.

I watched the skinhead's chest, checking for the rise and fall. Every breath he took was a gurgling, bubbly sound, the mixture of air and blood.

Woody's eyes shifted back and forth, from me to the skinhead and back. There was a trepidation, a sense of being unsure of what to do next. The sound of the genny and the shitty stereo and everything else in the world dropped out, and all I heard was breathing: my inhalation and exhaling, the skinhead's strained noises, and Woody in stasis, not seeming to breathe at all.

"Clock's ticking here, boss," I said.

Woody nodded. "Yeah. Yeah, it is." He came to his feet, kept his eyes on the skinhead.

"We ready to do this thing?"

"I am. You ready?"

The racking of the action on a shotgun echoed through the darkness. This was when I realized we had both let our backs go to the trailer, and we hadn't been paying attention to what was going on.

"Drop the gun," a man's voice called out behind us.

Woody looked at me. "Didn't cover our six, did you?"

"It would seem that I did not."

"How many back there, you suppose?"

"Well, we know one, and he's already dropped a shell in there, so he's ready."

"And he's in a good range, too. One shot would probably be enough, give us both sucking chest wounds."

"What other types of chest wounds are there? Getting shot in the chest would always suck."

Whoever was holding the shotgun cleared his throat. "Are you fuckers deaf? I said—"

"We know what you said," I said. "We're debating options here."

"I got a shotgun pointed at the back of your goddamn skulls," he said, his voice shaky. "Options are, you want shot in the head or the ass?"

Woody sighed and lowered his shotgun to the ground. I followed suit.

"Now turn around," the man said.

The guy holding the shotgun looked barely big enough to lift damn thing. His skin was red and blotchy, sores dotting his face. He wore an apron that read "Kiss the Cook." He was maybe mid-twenties, going on fifty.

"Oh look," I said. "He's got a shotgun, too."

"There was a sale at Walmart," Woody said. "More like in the parking lot of Walmart. Guy had 'em in his trunk."

"I guess you really can get everything there."

The guy with the gun wasn't laughing. He told us to lace our fingers together and place them on our heads and drop to our knees, the way he'd heard it said on cop shows. Like all good kids who don't want to die in the middle of nowhere at the hands of a tweaker holding an illegally modified firearm, we did as told.

The trailer door opened behind him and an older guy with a short white ponytail walked out, talking on a cell phone. "Don't know who they are," he said. "Yes, sir. We'll hold 'em until you get here."

143

Ponytail Guy ended the call and shoved the phone into his pocket and stuck his hand out to the tweaker. "Gimme the gun."

The tweaker's eyes danced like an epileptic doing the jitterbug. "Why? What am I giving you the gun for? I got this."

"Gimme the gun, Mossy."

Mossy didn't move. Okay, to be fair, he did move, but twitchiness didn't count as the moving Ponytail Guy wanted. Plus, his finger on the trigger kept jumping, which didn't fill me with confidence. I took a deep breath and consigned myself to being shot in the face. It would have been the perfect capstone to my day.

"Mossy," Ponytail Guy said. There wasn't room for debate in his tone.

Mossy handed the shotgun to Ponytail Guy, who aimed it at us again. "Need you to go inside, get me some pillowcases."

Mossy shifted to an almost-violent tremble. I felt safer with Ponytail Guy pointing the shotgun at us, and then I realized how fucked it was to have varying degrees of okay about having a gun pointed at you at all.

"Where...where...where they at?" Mossy said.

"On the pillows, dumb ass," Ponytail Guy said.

Mossy disappeared into the trailer. There was chattering inside, and the curtains parted and faces peered out.

"Get back to work in there," Ponytail Guy said without turning around. The curtains closed back. To us, he said, "Off with the masks, assholes."

Woody and I pulled off the masks.

To Woody, I said, "Doesn't it bother you they don't seem to care about their friend on the ground behind us you took the time to beat unconscious?"

"Everyone has different priorities," Woody said.

Ponytail Guy stepped back. "What are you assholes talking about?" He looked around us and seemed to notice the skinhead on the ground. "Did you kill Roger?"

Roger snorted a breath full of blood.

"He's alive," I said.

"Damn shame," Ponytail Guy said. "Though his Spotify list sucks."

"Won't be much of an issue here soon," I said. "We worked him over pretty good. He's not going to make it much longer."

"'We'?" Woody said. "Who's 'we' here? I didn't see you helping."

"What d'you beat him up so bad for?" Ponytail Guy said.

"He called you a goat-sucking faggot," I said. "I told him that was an insult to both gay men and goats. And probably gay goats."

Mossy came out of the trailer holding pillowcases. "What now?"

Ponytail Guy gestured toward us with what was left of the barrel of the shotgun. "Pat 'em down, see if they've got any guns on them."

Mossy walked to us, the pillowcases hanging in his hands. He dropped them to the ground and stood beside Woody. Woody didn't flinch.

"Stand up," Mossy said. The words didn't have much weight behind them, and Woody didn't respond. Mossy nudged at Woody with the toe of his shoe. "I said to stand up." He said it with more determination, like a toddler making demands of a parent. Still nothing. Mossy pushed at him harder with his foot. "Stand the fuck up."

Woody's movements were a blur. He was on his feet, one arm around Mossy's neck, his pistol in his other hand pressing against Mossy's right template. Mossy began to shake again. If he vibrated much harder, he'd slip dimensions.

Ponytail Guy swung the shotgun barrel toward Woody. "Drop the gun or I'll blow you both away right here."

There was a trickling sound. A puddle formed at Mossy's feet as urine ran from the cuff of his pants. The bitter chemical stink cut through the cold night air. I fought back the urge to retch.

145

Woody grounded himself, tightening his grip around Mossy's neck. What remained of Mossy's teeth chattered, and a constant stream of "fuckfuckfuckfuckfuck" spewed out between the rattling.

There was maybe six feet between Ponytail Guy and Woody. The shotgun stayed level on Woody, and by default, on Mossy. Mossy started crying.

I lowered my hands and moved to rise. My pistol was at the small of my back. If I could get to it soon enough...

"You go for a gun, and I'm shooting one of you sons-of-bitches," Ponytail Guy said, like he was reading my thoughts off a billboard. His eyes never left Woody and Mossy. His voice was level. No emotion.

I resumed the position.

A smile flickered across Woody's face. "Where were you?"

Ponytail Guy said, "Vietnam, '70 to '72, a few places after that. You?"

"Middle East shit, some stuff in Central America," Woody said. "Later, though. Toward the end of Reagan, and I hung around for most of Bush the Greater."

"Fun times. I heard good things. Shame I never got a piece of that."

"You didn't miss much, outside of the food."

"Everyone said the food was great. The pussy, not so much. Out of curiosity, you ever find it funny, the guys you trained in the Middle East, they were lobbing bombs and airplanes at us fifteen years later?"

"It's not 'Breakfast at Tiffany's,' but there's humor in it, sure."

Behind me, Roger gurgled out a breath. He drew in a raspy gasp and coughed and strangled out a noise meant to be a scream, but it caught somewhere in the clotting blood and came out more like a breeze whistling through a leaky window.

"Roger!" Ponytail Guy said.

Roger rolled his head to one side. "Mike," he said.

"How you doin' over there?" Ponytail Guy—or Mike, if you

146

prefer—said.

Roger coughed and gasped. "Been better. Fucked me over, the assholes."

"So I can tell." Mike walked toward Roger, keeping the shotgun pointed at Woody and Mossy. He paused in front of me and said, "Gimme your gun. And don't be stupid. Set it on the ground. One hand. Other hand stays on top of your head."

I lowered one hand and reached back and took my nine millimeter and laid it next to me. Mike turned the barrel of his shotgun toward me as he bent down and took my shotgun and threw it toward the trailer, then picked up the pistol and kept it hanging loose in his hand.

Mike stood up straight and moved closer to Roger. He kept the shotgun aimed at me. Woody twisted his body around to face Mike, bringing Mossy along for the ride. Mike stood over Roger.

"I'm gonna need help, Mike," Roger said. "I need a goddamn doctor. I…I can feel all this blood in my head…"

"It's gonna be good, don't you worry," Mike said.

Mike shot Roger in the face with the pistol. He didn't look down, never breaking eye contact with Woody. Roger's body jumped off the ground and landed hard. His head shattered and chunks of him scattered, and something hard and sharp flicked across my face, and I knew it was a shard of skull.

Woody didn't move.

Mike stepped over Roger's body and behind me. He put a foot to the back of my head and pushed until my face hit the ground. "Stay down," he said. I moved my head to where I could see him walking toward Woody.

"Let him go, or I'll just shoot him and then I'll shoot you," Mike said.

Woody weighed it for a second. You could see him calculating options and variables. He finished the mental math and pulled his arm away from Mossy's neck and let the pistol fall.

"On the ground," Mike said.

I got a mouthful of cold winter soil as Mossy said, "Oh fuck god thank—" followed by a shotgun blast.

The last thing I saw before the pillowcase went over my head was Mossy's body, bleeding from a dozen different places, twisted in a way it never should have been.

Mike tied my hands behind my back. I guessed he did the same thing to Woody, since I doubted I was that special.

I tried to not think about the smell on the pillowcase, or what I was breathing in through the material. I worked to not think about the endless number of minutes where I laid there on the ground with my face to the dirt, listening to Mike make phone calls, maybe waiting for the sound of a gunshot next to me and the end of Woody, followed by the gunshot I'd never hear. I struggled to not think about the two dead men who were footsteps away.

Mostly I tried to not think that maybe I should have died in that traffic stop outside of Morgantown, standing there in the rain. People had always seemed obliged to tell me I was lucky to be alive. Face down to the ground, waiting to see what would happen next, I didn't feel any of that luck, or much luck at all.

CHAPTER 31

No clue how much time passed before I heard tires crunch into the frozen ground. It sounded like pickup trucks. The engines shut off and people got out. Someone stopped, and I heard a kick and Woody grunted. A moment later a boot connected with my right side. The air rushed out of me, and I might have ached more if that were possible. There was the sound of a woman's laughter.

"It's too quiet," the woman said. "What kind of music you got into that shit shack?"

"Whatever you like, Ms. Mayhew," Mike said. He sounded softer, more subservient now, less the gun-wielding asshole. The district manager only has so much power once the company president shows up, I guess.

"Go surprise me," she said.

The trailer door opened and closed and then the Ramones blared from inside, "Blitzkrieg Bop." The woman said, "Very nice," and tapped her foot on the ground. She waited until the next song came on—The Voidoids and "Blank Generation"— before she said, "Stand 'em up and take the hoods off of 'em."

"They're pillowcases, Ms. Mayhew," Mike said. "We wouldn't waste good hoods on race traitors."

"Whatever. Just get 'em up off the ground."

They weren't gentle pulling us up as they yanked the pillowcases off. There were four men, all of them brandishing automatic weapons. They were an assortment of white guys with shaved heads, bad facial hair and white power tattoos. None of them looked like they kept up with current events or were a few credits shy on their graduate work.

The woman was nearly six feet tall, hair so blonde it was almost white, cut in a longish bob, and dressed all in black, including driving gloves, an ankle-length wool coat, and boots with four-inch heels. She smiled a mouthful of the most even, white teeth I'd ever seen.

"So," she said, still smiling, "which one of you cocksuckers is Henry Malone?"

"He is," Woody said without missing a beat.

The blonde walked up to me. She smelled like expensive perfume you would not find at the Parker County Walmart. Closer up, I could see how taut her skin was, drawn tight over high cheekbones, and her eyes had a feverish wildness that shone in the moonlight. She was scary as shit, the chick you weren't sure would fuck you or kill you, and depending on the circumstance, you wouldn't care. This wasn't one of those circumstances.

"Do you know who I am?" she said. Her pupils were pin-pricks that danced in the darkness.

"The Lindbergh baby?"

She laughed. "Try again."

"Winner of 'Best Interracial Anal Scene' at the 2015 Adult Film Awards? Because if so, I love your work."

She laughed again, with less enthusiasm and fewer teeth this time. "Once again," she said, almost purring. "With emotion this time."

"Probably not someone who swallows?"

She belted me. Right hook, connected with the jaw. My vision blurred. Cartoon bluebirds circled my head for a second. There was way more muscle behind that punch than I had expected.

She massaged her fist with her other hand. "I am Monica Mayhew. You may be familiar with me."

"I've heard of you," I said. I shifted my jaw back and forth, making sure nothing was broken. "I was wrong about that part where you don't swallow, then."

She hit me again. This one wasn't as unbridled as before, and I was more prepared for it, but it still hurt. I sucked cold air into my lungs and shifted my weight to keep steady,

She took a step back from me. The tail of the overcoat waved like a cape, and I bet she'd practiced that move, trying to look cool. It worked. "Just so you know, I can keep this up as long as you can, and when I get tired, I'll have someone else beat the fuck out of you."

My ears rang, and there wasn't two of everything, but nothing was solid either, slipping into ghostly images before sliding back into itself. I watched the Casper version of Monica Mayhew pace back and forth in front of me, looking like a business-minded dominatrix.

She made clicking noises with her tongue. "Mr. Malone, this isn't the part of the movie where you and I will exchange witty unpleasantries with one another." She reached underneath her coat and brought out a revolver, pressed the barrel against my forehead, and cocked the hammer. The metal felt cold and weirdly refreshing. "This is the part of the movie where you'll tell me what I want to know, or I'll shoot you in the head."

"Go for it," I said. "But you'll be amazed at all the shit I don't know."

Her blood-red lips drew into a smile. She brought the gun away from my forehead and walked over to Woody and pushed the barrel just above his ear. Woody never moved. Her smile got cockier.

"Then let's say I kill your friend here," she said. "What do you say that about that?"

"I say, 'I'll avenge your death, Woody.'"

Woody said, "Much appreciated." He otherwise maintained his Easter Island aesthetic.

Monica Mayhew pulled the gun back, flipped it in the air,

caught it by the barrel, and smashed the grip across Woody's head. He wobbled but worked to seem unfazed. She re-holstered the weapon and found a position where Woody and I could both see her. She put her hands on her hips, elbows out, face full of determination, like a Valkyrie, except out of her goddamn mind.

"Why do you insist in making this all so goddamn difficult?" she said. "You're already responsible for the deaths of two men tonight, and the likelihood of me killing you is high, so explain why you want to add being pains in the ass on top of everything else."

I jerked my head in Mike's direction. "Sgt. Slaughter over there was the one blowing your guys away. Not us."

"I'm aware of how those men died. The Brotherhood doesn't tolerate failure, and neither Mr. Thompson nor Mr. Moss fit into our long-term business goals."

Woody laughed. The sound was like cold air blasting in your face

"Mr. Arbogast," Monica Mayhew said to Woody, turning to him. Woody's eyebrows lifted. "I'm well aware of who you are, as I was aware also of who Mr. Malone is. I asked only to see who would be most willing to self-identify, and who would be most willing to sell the other one out."

"I'm not selling anyone out," Woody said. "You asked a question earlier, and I answered it. I was taught it was polite to answer a lady's questions, even if she's a fucking pinhead. And as far as not accepting failure as an option, I've got to tell you, honey, these slant-skulled motherfuckers you call 'followers' are so accustomed to failure, they wouldn't even make it to leave the money on the dresser first before the hour started."

Monica Mayhew pushed close into Woody's face. Much closer, and their eyeballs would have touched. "It's a shame you don't see the greater purpose of what the Brotherhood is trying to accomplish, Mr. Arbogast."

Woody spit on the ground. More of it was blood than saliva.

"Don't act like you're feeding the hungry, or buying coats for the homeless. You're selling drugs to buy guns because your paranoid inbreds are scared of dark-skinned people. You want a gold star for that?"

She walked over to Woody. "No, Mr. Arbogast, I do not. What I want is for you to see that what we're doing will save your stupid cracker ass from the mongrel nations that threaten to—"

"Jesus Christ on a crispy cracker, are you going to shoot us or monologue us to death?" Woody said. "Because if it's the monologue, you can shoot me instead."

Monica Mayhew drove the toe of her left boot into Woody's nuts. Woody grunted and his body doubled over. He strained to hold it all in as his face reddened and his eyes swelled. Monica Mayhew brought her foot back, ready to kick Woody's grape sack back inside him.

I moved like I was about to charge forward. Monica Mayhew caught sight of the motion and stopped. One of the skinheads saw me also, and he stepped up and smacked me across the face with the butt of his rifle. The blow dropped me hard, sent me backwards. There was a cracking noise I suspected was my nose breaking. I landed on my ass. I struggled to catch my breath, everything so fast and painful my brain couldn't process it fast enough. My face felt warm and wet. Blood. Yep, there was my nose. Fuck.

I rolled onto my front and brought myself up onto my knees. Blood dripped off my chin. I burped and tasted bile.

I pushed my good leg and knee out and sucked in some air, bracing for the roar of pain that would come when I tried to bend my other knee. I bit down on the inside of the cheek, and I wasn't disappointed when I moved my other knee. The hurt shot through any nerve it could reach in my body like angry lightning. My eyes rolled backwards, and I grunted and groaned until I was standing upright.

Monica Mayhew did the sarcastic show handclap. "How

fucking heroic of you, Mr. Malone. Your perseverance is admirable. It's a shame you're a goddamn retard, though."

I spit out a mouthful of blood. "I would tell you to fuck off, Mayhew, but you caught me on a day where I'm fresh out of fucks to give."

The skinhead who'd so kindly broken my nose brought his rifle back to clock me again when Monica Mayhew said, "Stop." The skinhead froze in mid-movement and dropped his weapon to his side. She walked over in front of me. Her eyes met mine. They were feral, hungry eyes. Her appeal made a sick sense in that moment, and I could see why Walters had fucked her, though Walters would probably fuck anything with a pulse, and I wasn't sure about the pulse.

She licked her lips. They gleamed in the moonlight. Next, she'd try to tie a cherry stem into a knot with her tongue. I'd bet it was a party trick that worked on men she didn't smack around. Or the smacking around came later; I didn't judge. Yet, for some odd reason, perhaps the sensation of warm, thick blood dribbling down my face, or the dead bodies a few feet away, I wasn't getting stirred up in my nether regions.

"You're not my type," I said. "I go for a different kind for psycho, but thanks anyway. The ones who aren't racist lunatics."

She looked taken aback. Maybe she wasn't used to it not working. "Oh well. Make this as difficult as you like. I don't care."

"I'm unclear what the hell this is," I said. "You're buying guns for what reason? You think you'll take back the nation? I hate to break it to you, but as soon as you as your moron masses opt to attack, there's gonna be a swarm of tanks and drones that'll turn you all into red mist. You fuckers have fun with that."

She reached out and ran a finger along my jaw. I shook off her touch. She grabbed me by the neck and gave a good squeeze, thumb denting into my carotid enough to let me know it was there.

"Nothing so plebeian as that, Mr. Malone" Her voice shifted into something just beyond a growl. "What you're suggesting is passive, and short-sighted. What we will do is a wholesale change of thought for every right-minded man, woman and child in the nation. See, the guns that Mr. Walters helped us buy, we're going to make sure they find their way into every major inner city. Every crack smoker, every wetback, every brownskin that has worked to push out the white way of life, is going to find himself armed. And then, Mr. Malone, we, the Brotherhood, we do nothing. We wait for the bullets to start flying, and for people to die."

She pressed harder on the big artery and pushed her palm into my windpipe and I felt myself getting lightheaded. I focused on her words, on staying in the moment. "At first, it won't be anyone important, just niggers and spics and ragheads, wiping one another out, but as they get braver, they'll move on and out and they'll find themselves in suburbs and the white enclaves of America, and when white people start dying at the hands of inner city street trash, that is when people will care what's happening. Then, the Brotherhood will be there to help instruct people on what to do, on how to keep themselves safe, and that race war we've been waiting for for generations, it will be here. White America will rise up and reclaim itself. The white, Christian nation that America was meant to be will again reassert itself as the rightful leader of this world."

She loosened her grip on my throat. What blood I wasn't wearing rushed toward my brain. "Anyway, I suspect that grand plans aren't anything small-minded thinkers such as yourself care about. Perhaps we can move on to what's important."

"Thank Jesus," Woody said. "A point." There was a lot of pain in his voice, not that I could blame him.

Monica Mayhew ignored Woody. She said, "You were look-ing for Bobbi Fisher, is that correct?"

I shook my head, not as a response to her but to move the

blood in my head around. "You've got this annoying tendency toward asking questions you already know the answers to."

"Those are always the best ones to ask. There's less guesswork. We'll move on to a question I don't have the answer and you sure as fuck had better hope you do." She patted me on the cheek. "Where's the three hundred thousand dollars that cunt stole?"

CHAPTER 32

"Three. Hundred. Thousand. Dollars." She spoke each word as if it were its own thought. "Bobbi Fisher was fucking Richard Walters, and when she disappeared, so did three hundred thousand dollars of the Brotherhood's money from his possession."

Just when you think shit can't get worse...

"We don't know anything about any money," I said.

"You should, because you are aware of the whereabouts of Ms. Fisher, and she has our money," Monica Mayhew said. "It's simple: she gives us back our money, and almost everyone gets to live."

"We're talking about cash from your meth operation, aren't we?"

"Where the money came from is irrelevant, Mr. Malone. What matters is it's gone, and we want it back."

She wagged a finger at the skinhead. Nodded to him. I braced myself for it, but don't kid yourself that there's ever a way to be ready for a rifle butt to the stomach. He rammed it hard into my gut. I pushed back what would be a spray of vomit and instead hocked up and spat out a glob of something that might have been my spleen.

Monica Mayhew watched it with bland interest, like the preparation of a meal she wasn't hungry for. She rested her hands on her hips.

My knee chose then to not want to work anymore, and I

157

stumbled forward. I caught myself in time, dropped to the knee, and screamed under my breath. I took a breath and stood up. Real. Fucking. Slowly. Guns raised and aimed at me. I gritted my teeth and tried to muster up a Sylvester Stallone/"Rambo"-era tone.

"Go to hell," I said.

Monica Mayhew sighed. "Do you insist on continuing to be the tough guy, Mr. Malone? There's no profit in it, and frankly you're not good at it."

I pulled in air through my mouth since my nose had clotting blood in the way. "Let me reiterate, that you can go to hell."

"Fine, fine, fine. Let's try another tact." She tapped one of her soldiers on the shoulder. "From the van." He nodded and ran past me to an old panel van. "Tell me how you found the location of this cook house?"

The bottom fell out of my stomach and a fresh wave of nausea whipped through me as the skinhead pushed someone past me. Earl Teller had his hands tied behind his back and duct tape wrapped around his eyes and mouth. The skinhead positioned him in front of Monica Mayhew, pushing him down onto his knees.

"It wasn't difficult to piece it together," she said. "Instinctually, you know who will be strong, who will be weak. Jesus could tell who would betray him long before it happened."

Monica Mayhew ripped the duct tape from over Teller's eyes. His scream was strained through the tape over his mouth, but it was still audible, and it paled in comparison to what he let out when she took the duct tape off of his mouth. He looked as though he'd lost a bar fight with an entire bar. His eyes were swollen shut, his face puffy and misshapen, trails of dried blood mapping every contour.

She patted him on the head. "People tend to be friendly toward the Brotherhood, and they're willing to share when someone strays and drives off with someone they should not be associating with."

Teller looked pathetic. His eyes met mine. They were mournful, contrite, regretful he had spoken to me, or met me. I puffed out my chest and worked to sound like I didn't give a shit.

"Forgive me if I'm not broken-hearted because you knocked around an asshole who beat the fuck out of me," I said.

She walked around Teller, surveying him like livestock. "We had suspicions about where Mr. Teller's true loyalties might lie. He seemed to have an affinity for the tastes of inferior cultures."

"You mean he listens rap music."

"It's a slippery slope, Mr. Malone, from poor music choices to betraying the cause which will set you free." She propped an arm up on Teller and leaned against him. "When you and Mr. Arbogast showed up tonight, it didn't take long to put the puzzle together. We couldn't assume, though, so we had to make sure we were right. Eventually, Mr. Teller was forthcoming about what he told you that night." She snapped her fingers, and another skinhead broke away and ran back to the van. He came back a moment later with a rusted gas can and emptied its contents all over Teller.

Teller gagged and sputtered as he doused him down, scream-ing when the gas entered one of the hundred open wounds on his face. The skinhead cracked the can against Teller's head. He emptied the can, shaking to get the last drops out, and handed an old Zippo cigarette lighter to Monica Mayhew.

I didn't even try to stop myself. I lunged forward and vomited. It came in waves, pausing long enough for me to get my breath before another round arrived. Tears streamed down my cheeks, and my mouth burned as strings of acidic spit ran down my chin and neck.

Monica Mayhew looked as me as if I were a disappointing puppy who'd just dropped a shit on the rug. "You must not have the stomach for the costs of war," she said.

"This isn't a fucking war," I said, my voice wet and strained.

"But it is, Mr. Malone." Her voice was so fucking calm, prac-ticed. Akin to explaining the warranty options for a vacuum

159

cleaner. "We're in a war for the survival of our race. There are people streaming over our border by the thousands daily, thousands more in sand-infested shitholes training to murder us, and their only goal is nothing less than to take from us the lives we've worked to have, and I, for one, refuse to allow that. You do what you have to do."

She flicked the lighter, and a flame rose from it. She closed the lid, the flame disappeared, and she repeated the action, over and over and over, the click and pop of the lighter lid rhythmic.

"I will ask you again: where's the three hundred thousand Bobbi Fisher stole?" she said.

I blinked, trying to push away the tears, but it didn't work, and the flame became a soft blue light held aloft by a silhouette.

"I don't know." Puke and slobber dripped off of me. The stink was terrible.

"Bullshit. If you wait for us to find her, there will be casualties beyond anything you can imagine. I'll paint walls with blood if I have to. If she hasn't told you where the money is, I'd recommend you find out, or it's going to get very unpleasant, Mr. Malone."

"What makes you so sure she has the money?"

"Because she's the only loose end left. Plus, she's stupid enough of a cunt to believe she can get away with this. Trust me that she will not. I'm aware of her two precious daughters, and if she doesn't see fit to return what's ours, those girls will vanish, and she'll wonder for the rest of her pathetic life what happened to them. Then think about your own father, Mr. Malone. He's an old man. He doesn't have much longer for this world, but that time will get significantly shorter." She turned to Woody. "As for you, that pack of mutts you keep, they'll litter your lawn like cut grass."

Woody kept a blank expression. That's never good.

I said, "You'll get your goddamn money."

"Wonderful," she said. "Everyone can return to their dull little lives of quiet desperation." She shut the lid on the lighter. She held it in her hand, contemplating it. "Though there's still this matter of betrayal. It's vital that the stakes are understood by everyone." She flicked the lighter again. Nothing. Again. Still nothing. Again. This time the flame erupted from it.

She looked at Teller. "We'll say you were a martyr for a greater cause," she said as she threw the lighter to her feet. The gas ignited, and she walked away.

Flames rolled up and around Teller and crawled across his body. The night glowed an angry orange. He went from being a human being to a fireball in the time it took to blink, falling backward and trying to roll to put out the fire. Maybe he tried to scream, and couldn't. All I heard was the crackling sound of fire, consuming the gasoline, Teller's clothes, Teller himself.

I toppled over trying to stand. Two skinheads were on top of me as I tried to get up. I struggled. They caught me with easy blows to the gut, taking the fight out of me.

The fetor of burning fuel and charred flesh smothered me, and I would have given anything for the stink of vomit instead. Woody was still on his knees, expressionless as he watched the flaming sight that had once been Teller.

Teller burned for a while. It was long enough he stopped moving and the initial brightness from the gasoline faded, replaced by a steady flame.

Monica Mayhew nodded to a soldier. He walked over to what remained of Teller, unzipped his pants, whipped out his dick, and pissed into the flames. The flames hissed, and acrid steam rose and filtered its way through the air, and I wanted to puke again. One by one, the rest of the skinheads walked over and pissed on Teller's burning corpse.

I tried to turn my head. Monica Mayhew told a skinhead to put me in a headlock.

"There is a price for everything," she said. "Watch this and understand it."

The skinhead held me where I was, and I stared as the fire that was Earl Teller burned until there was nothing but a glow, and what was left was roughly human in shape, charred black, nothing but charcoal and ashes.

The skinheads kept me held down. I rolled my eyes up to look at the night sky. The moon was full and bright, half hidden behind clouds that blotted out the stars. I thought about Maggie, and nights we'd spent drinking and staring at the moon on the back deck of the shitty little house we'd rented in Morgantown. The place had a spite fence, and if the weather was warm, and we had enough to drink, we'd make love on the deck, knowing the neighbors couldn't see us but we made enough noise, they damn well knew we were there. We didn't care, though, because there wasn't anything else in the world just then but us. I tried to will myself back to one of those moments, to force time to unwind and pull me away from this.

It didn't work. Monica Mayhew's voice broke my thoughts. "Untie his hands," she said, crouching low. Her face was so close, it blotted out the moon. No emotion. Not anger, happy, sadness. Nothing.

"No one leaves this life without wounds, Mr. Malone," she said. "We are only as interesting as our scars. How interesting do you find yourself to be, Mr. Malone?"

She extended a hand and a skinhead next to her gave her a set of pruning clippers. To the skinhead holding my left arm, she said, "His hand."

I stiffened my arm and tried to pull away. Sweat raced from every available pore. The skinhead shifted from a headlock to a half Nelson. The skinhead with my left arm pushed at the outside of the joint and made my arm bend.

I wanted to fight more, but I couldn't. I had nothing left. So I just gave up. It was easier than I thought it would be.

Monica Mayhew grabbed my hand and selected my ring finger, slipping it between the clipper blades. "So far, I've found you hopelessly boring," she said. "I hope you become much more interesting after this."

She pressed on the handles. I heard the blades as they clicked and snapped together. They didn't go all the way through, and instead only took out bits of muscle and cartilage.

I screamed, and jerked away again, but I had even less in me at this point. There aren't words to describe that feeling. At first there wasn't a feeling, the blade sharp, but then it hit me, and I screamed again.

"The song was wrong," Monica Mayhew said. "The first cut wasn't the deepest. Guess we'll have to go again."

There was another clipping sound, and I screamed again, and began to cry.

CHAPTER 33

I woke up to the smell of coffee and bacon frying, and to the sound of Earl Teller dying filling my ears.

I snapped into consciousness and shot upright in bed and realized this wasn't my bedroom. The room was blank and empty, nothing but a bed and a dresser. Everything sparse and functional. I must be at Woody's house.

I wore a Cincinnati Reds T-shirt and jeans with the cuffs rolled up an inch thick. This was Woody's clothes, since the bastard was a half-foot taller than me, and thought Pete Rose's exclusion from Cooperstown was a crime akin to Watergate.

I had a moment where everything felt like it was all a dream. That I'd gone on a bender and imagined the trailer and the skinheads, and Monica Mayhew, and Teller going out in a blinding flash of hydrocarbons—

Then I saw my left hand, layered underneath bandages, and the empty spot where my ring finger should have been.

I leaned over the side of the bed and vomited. It was clear and watery, tapping into emergency reserves since I'd emptied my stomach's contents so efficiently at the cookhouse.

Woody had left a bucket for me. I kept it contained somehow. My one small victory in this entire clusterfuck.

I shuffled into the kitchen and sat down at the table. Woody was at the stove, flipping bacon. He filled a coffee cup from the percolator and set it at the table, then set in front of me a plate of bacon and scrambled eggs big enough to feed a battalion. From the refrigerator he got cheese and salsa and placed them nearby.

I looked at the food and, for a moment, couldn't imagine eating any of it, or anything else, ever again. I'd stopped eating pork years ago after watching a documentary that showed pigs are smarter and dogs. I figured that since I couldn't eat a dog, it didn't seem fair to eat anything smarter than it. My stomach did an involuntary rumble anyway because, let's face it, bacon smells great.

I dumped an ungodly amount of cheese and salsa on the eggs and ate with a slow, methodical pace. Woody took a chair and drank his coffee. I wiped out the eggs but left the bacon where it was, pushing the plate aside.

He gestured toward the bacon. 'I respect the 'pigs are smart' thing, but you need the protein."

"I'm thinking about laying off cooked flesh for a while."

"Can't say I blame you. The whole situation went tits-up rather fast."

"That's one way to put it." I sipped from a water glass next to my plate. "Where's Bobbi?"

"She's in bed. She got a little hysterical when I brought you in covered in blood."

"Just like a woman to go to pieces over the littlest things."

Woody snatched a piece of my bacon and whistled. Four dogs barreled into the room, squealing to a stop in front of him. He said something that sounded German and they all sat down. He said something else, and they rose onto their hind legs, front paws reaching into the air. Another command had them back on all four. He took three more pieces of bacon and positioned a piece of bacon at the end of each of their snouts. No one moved, just there with eyes focused on bacon as it teeter-tottered on their snouts.

He gave another command, and each dog popped their heads

up, sending the bacon flying, and snatching it in mid-air before devouring it. They stared at Woody, four sets of big brown eyes, hoping for more. He gave them another order, and they headed out the door, back to doing whatever a pack of dogs does when not begging for food.

Woody ate the last strip of bacon from my plate. My stomach flopped around and I pushed back my eggs.

"They let you waltz out of there with me without a fight?" I said.

"They did, but they reiterated the urgency to produce the three hundred grand for them in a timely manner, and then they said to get you to the hospital before you bled to death."

"I can't help but notice this isn't a hospital."

"Taking you to Parker General and explaining the night's events wasn't the best idea ever." He gestured to my bandaged hand. "Besides, it was a clean cut, and easy stitches."

"Modern medicine can reattach fingers."

"If there's a finger to reattach."

"They kept my finger?"

"They did."

"Why the fuck did they keep my finger?"

"I'm not sure, Henry. Why did the psycho skinheads do something inexplicable? Because everything else they've done so far follows patterns of common sense, human courtesy, and concern for the law."

I sighed. "Fair point and thank you. You come out unscathed?"

"I came home fully intact."

"Ain't you the lucky fucker?"

"Considered hitting the slot machines on the way home, I felt so lucky." He laid his hand on his crotch and winced. "Surprised she didn't rupture me with that pointy-toed boot to the balls."

I leaned back in my chair. "I feel the elephant on the table now is the three hundred grand, isn't it?"

"I asked Bobbi. She doesn't know what they're talking about."

"You believe her?"

"I do." His tone was that I should as well.

Bobbi cleared her throat. She stood in the doorway, looking small and pale and scared. Woody rose and walked toward her. She drew a step backward, and he stopped and she looked at me and bit at her bottom lip. It seemed as if she was about to say something, but she froze with her mouth open, and turned and walked out. The porch door squeaked open and then slammed shut.

I reached out to Woody as he headed in that direction. "Let me talk to her," I said.

He nodded. "Sure."

Woody's front porch stared over the empty fields of farmland. Sunlight glistened off of old snow. A breeze moved bits of white powder around in whirling wisps.

Bobbi wasn't wearing a coat. She leaned against a porch rail and smoked a cigarette and shivered. I sat down in a wooden rocking chair.

She said, "Fuck, but I hate my life."

"I don't blame you."

She did a slow turn and burn at me, her blue eyes feral and angry. "You're an asshole."

"I get a lot of that. But hey, you don't want agreed with, don't make statements like that."

She glanced down at my left hand. "Fuck."

I flipped my hand back and forth. "I'm not thrilled about it, either. On the plus side, though, it'll be a lot easier to flip people off with one less finger to worry about."

She took a last drag on her cigarette before tossing it into a sand bucket Woody kept on the porch, then lit a fresh Marlboro Light from a pack of cigarettes in her pocket.

"I have dated the wrong men, fucked the even wronger men, and done nothing but make bad decisions, but until now, I'm the only one getting hurt. The girls, they've dodged the bullets, it felt like. Then this shit happens." She shook her head. "What the hell?"

I stood and took a position against the railing next to her. She held her cigarettes out toward me. "You want one?"

I took one, and the lighter she offered. On the inhale I thought I might die. It tasted like shit, but then again, anyone who said they smoked for the taste was a lying motherfucker. It was nicotine, and I wasn't concerned about much else.

Her eyes drifted toward the door. "Woody, he's the first man to treat me like a lady, not just a chick to fuck."

"He's a good man, that one. I'd snatch him up for myself if he was so inclined, and I was similarly inclined."

"That's a lot of inclining."

"I'm not sure either one of us have that much inclination in us." I took another drag and exhaled. "Why do you think the Brotherhood thinks you've got their money?"

"I'll guess it's because Richie told them I have it. Except, if I had taken it, I wouldn't even fucking be here right now. I'd have grabbed my girls and gone, and wouldn't have given a shit. But when I vanished, maybe Richie figured this would be a chance to use me as an excuse to take some cash for himself did something with the money, and then point a finger at me."

I lifted my hand in the air. "Wonder if he's got one extra he can spare."

There was shock on her face in the first seconds, as the words hung there in the cold air. but the shock melted into laughter. Her face flushed red, and she covered her mouth to hide her laughing.

She finished a good chuckle at my expense and wiped tears from her eyes. "Mind if I ask you a question, since it seems nothing's off limits with you?"

"Ask away."

"How did you get that limp?"

I took a deep breath.

"A few years back, I was working radar on a stretch of I-68

outside of Morgantown, headed towards Maryland. It was a Wednesday evening, a nothing kind of night, and I'd tagged folks and gotten grief from them, the usual shit about how I had nothing else to do but pull over good, law-abiding folks who happened to be going twenty over the speed limit.

"Dark clouds rolled in from the west and the sky opened up this torrential downpour, and that will more than not slow folks down. I planned to close up shop as this car came out of nowhere, doing ninety easy. It was a Ford Mustang, late model, beautiful fucking car, and it zipped by me. A car going that fast, in those conditions, is a recipe for an accident. I radioed it in and flipped my lights on and jumped into pursuit.

"The rain came down harder and harder, and he was flying in and out of traffic, dodging cars and eighteen wheelers. Vehicles pulled over because the weather was getting worse, and I pushed it to cut that distance between us. The highway was slick, visibility was bad, it was a shitty situation, but all I saw was this guy causing a wreck, people getting hurt, people getting killed, so I stayed on his ass, because that's what I'm supposed to do, keep people safe.

"We must have raced liked this for five or six miles, which is nothing when you're hitting eighty-five, ninety miles an hour, when he pulled over. Used his fucking signal. Driving like a maniac and used a signal to pull over.

"I put on my hat and got out of my cruiser and approached the vehicle. The rain, it was pounding on me. Sky was black. I had my hand on my gun because I didn't know what I was walking into.

"The driver's door flew open and this guy, a skinny piece of shit, got out and swung a shotgun toward me and he fired. The blast caught me in my right knee, and I dropped like a rock, screaming. The reports I read after it happened said I drew my gun and opened fire. I emptied the magazine into him. Fifteen shots. I have no memory of that. Found out later the guy was a meth head who had killed his girlfriend earlier in the day after she refused to give him thirty bucks so he could get high. He stole the car from the neighbors and planned to trade it to his dealer for a hit.

"The next thing I do remember was waking up in the hospital and being told how my right knee was destroyed, and I was getting a complete replacement, and there went my days of walking like a normal human being. Said I'd have a hell of a hobble for the rest of my life, and they were not shitting about that. I had a shit-ton of the surgeries—I lost count after a point—and I never put a state trooper uniform on again.

"The state police gave me the options of taking a desk job or early retirement with disability. I knew I couldn't clock a desk job for the next twenty years, so I took retirement. And here I am, disabled with a state pension. I am living the dream, Bobbi. The motherfucking dream."

I exhaled.

Bobby kept a watch on the fields. "Damn, son, but you're broken goods."

I opened my mouth to reply when Woody poked his head out the door.

"Sheriff's on your cell phone, Henry, wanting to talk to you."

CHAPTER 34

Simms told me to come to Walters' house. He wouldn't say why, only to haul my ass there and don't spare the horses. He asked if I needed directions. I told him I did not, and I cut him off before he had a chance to ask me why.

I washed myself off at the bathroom sink because I couldn't navigate the shower one-handed, and I tried to make myself presentable; it was an abysmal failure. My face was swollen and bruised, and my clothes were still filthy with blood and mud, and I wasn't sure anyone had enough soap to get me to wear them again. Woody loaned me a flannel shirt, which hung on me like someone had washed me in hot water and dried me on high heat.

We left Bobbi on the couch surrounded by several of Woody's larger guns and dogs both. She looked safer than I felt.

Woody drove, on the theory that since I'd just woken up from shock-induced sleep following the hacking off of a digit, maybe I shouldn't be operating a motor vehicle. Yet another reason he was the brains of the operation.

A thin column of smoke rose from the general direction of Walters' house. County and state police cars and fire trucks lined the subdivision street.

The burned-out remains of a car sat in Walters' driveway. I recognized what was left of it as Earl Teller's excuse for a ride. A sheriff's deputy opened the trunk, looked inside, made a face, and ran into Walters' yard to vomit.

A state trooper stepped in front of us as we headed toward the driveway. "Crime scene, guys. Need to back off."

Thompson was talking to Simms near Teller's car when he saw us and motioned for us. "Let 'em through." The trooper stepped to one side.

Simms and Thompson stood at the front door. Both looked fatigued to the points of near-exhaustion. Their expressions said I hadn't been called out because they missed my company.

Simms looked at my hand. "What happened to you?"

"I cut myself shaving."

"You shaving your hands?"

"Just my palms. I'm single and I get lonely."

Simms looked at Woody. "And who are you?"

I'm the comedic sidekick," Woody said. "Name's Woody."

"That a first name or a last name?"

"Name's Woody," he said again.

They walked us to the front porch. "When was the last time you saw Earl Teller?" Simms said. He pointed at the smoldering automotive remains in the driveway. "I'm asking because that car belongs to him."

"It's a lovely car," I said.

"With a body burned up in the trunk. Body's more cooked than the car is. We're pretty sure it's Teller's body." He took a wallet out of his coat pocket. "Teller's wallet, with his ID. Someone chucked it into Walters' front yard before they doused the car in gas and set the whole thing on fire about three a.m. this morning."

"You don't need to say 'this morning' when you say 'three a.m.'" I said. "The 'a.m.' gives that part away. It's like saying 'ATM machine,' because the 'M' already stands for 'machine'—"

Simms propped himself against the porch, arms folded across his chest. "Malone, my deputy already wants to snap you in two, half on sheer principle and half out of sheer boredom, so I'd recommend you keep your mouth shut for a while."

I nodded. "Sound advice."

Woody said, "You getting anything out of Richie Walters about this?"

"He claims nothing but abject ignorance, which isn't hard to believe," Simms said. "Says the noise woke him up. He saw the car on fire in his driveway and called 911." Simms adjusted his stance. "You have anything to do with his alleged assault the other day? He says he was robbed, but never bothered to a report."

I smiled. "While I'd love to tune that motherfucker like a piano, I regret to say none of that was on me. But it's an odd thing, how he had this mysterious beating and then someone burns a car in his driveway with a white supremacist dead in the trunk already."

"Once may argue someone's trying to send him a message."

"A telegram is a message, Sheriff; you burn someone alive, you're taking it to another level."

Simms furrowed his eyebrows. "Why d'you say that?"

I realized I'd stepped right into it.

"Say what?"

"You said they burned someone alive; why you say it like that? He might have been dead when they shoved him in the trunk."

I heard the seconds tick by with every heartbeat pulsing in my ears.

"I'm spitballing here, Sheriff. He might have been alive when they set the car on fire. When you do shit like this, you might as well go big."

Simms nodded. "You still looking into the Bobbi Fisher thing?"

I took a deep breath. Simms wasn't stupid. It would have been easier if he was. I didn't know how long I wanted to keep compounding lies to him.

"I'm poking around at it," I said.

"Found out anything new?"

"Not really. Things sort of petered out."

Simms studied me for a while. Finally, he said, "You want to go inside, have a talk with Walters?"

I rubbed my hands together. My left hand ached sharply and suddenly. I looked at it and stared at the empty spot where my finger should have been. For a moment, there wasn't anything but this hand that felt like mine, but it wasn't, and somehow it had detached from me, and I stared at it, wondering where it came from.

Noises swirled in my ears. I thought they were human voices, but I couldn't process them. Something flicked at my earlobe, and it hurt. I jerked and remembered where I was. Woody pointed at Simms.

"Sheriff's talking to you," he said.

Simms stared at me like I was a science fair project, or an exhibit at the zoo.

"You okay?" he said.

"I'm fucking awesome," I said. "Let's go chat Richie the fuck up."

CHAPTER 35

Walters' house was full of bad art, wall-to-wall carpet, and antique family photos that weren't really his family. We passed a rec room with a pool table with a dark green, unscarred felt surface, and deer heads hanging on the wall.

The living room had a seventy-inch flat screen, overstuffed chairs, and James Patterson novels on the shelves. Mrs. Walters was seated, dressed a pink running suit, her big blonde hair pulled back into a ponytail. She looked as though she'd been crying for a while. Walters was at a bar, pouring whiskey into a tumbler filled with ice. His bruises had faded to yellow, and he was less swollen, but he still moved stiffly, like his clothing was too tight in all the wrong places.

When we walked in, Mrs. Walters' attention went straight to Simms. His body language loosened, and his eyes softened. She put her arms around him and sniffled.

Simms cradled her close to him. It wasn't impossible to imagine them years ago, still in love. It was almost too intimate to observe, and I tried to find something else in the room to look at.

"The state police are almost done taking pictures, and then they'll haul it away," Simms said.

Rachel rested her head on his shoulder. "Who does something like that? Something so sick."

Walters laughed. "Shit happens all the time in the real world, Rachel," he said, taking a drink of his whiskey. "Junkies and meth heads and liberals, they see what you've got and they think they can scare you into giving it to them."

All of that relaxation in Simms vanished at the sound of Walters' voice, and Simms broke away from his ex, his body readying for a fight. His hands curled into fists. Tendons stretched taut along his neck.

"So what you're saying, Mr. Walters," Simms said, "is you don't feel that this incident is related to your work?"

"Fuck no. People know who I am, and all they're looking for is an easy way to make money. They set stuff on fire in your driveway and think you'll stay awake all night with worry. The hell with that. We used to set couches on fire in Morgantown because WVU won a football game." He motioned toward the front of the house with the hand holding the whiskey glass. Globs of liquid splashed out of the glass and splattered across the carpet. I guessed this wasn't his first drink of the morning. "They're gonna have to do a hell of a lot better than that."

Rachel Walters seemed to realize there were people in the room other than her husband and Simms. She tilted her head as she looked at me, like a puppy struggling to understand a new trick. "You're the gentleman who brought Dickie home that night?"

I couldn't help but smile. "'Dickie'?" I pointed at Walters. "You're 'Dickie'? Are you 'Little Dickie' when the shower gets cold?"

Rachel Walters shook her head. Confusion settled in like morning fog. "You said you weren't a friend of his," she said to me. To Simms, she said, "Matty, what's going on?"

Simms looked at Thompson. "Carl, why don't you take Mrs. Walters to the station, maybe stop on the way and get a bite to eat or some coffee—"

She looked at Matt with a nine-year-old's version of anger. "Stop trying to protect me, Matty."

"'Matty'?" I said. It kept getting better.

"Rachel, please, I'm just—"

Walters sneered and dropped his voice an octave. "'Yes, Rachel, I'm trying to be the hero, Rachel.'" He topped off his drink and emptied half of the glass in a long swallow. "'I'm the sheriff. I've got to be the hero.'"

"Mr. Walters—" Simms said, not even bothering to hide the edge.

"Suck my dick, Sheriff, you and your 'Mr. Walters' shit. That you used to fuck my wife doesn't mean you get to call her 'Rachel' and then I'm 'Mr. Walters.' I hear how you sound when you say it. Like you found gum and dog shit on the bottom on your shoe." He pointed at me. "And what is this asshole doing here? He almost assaulted me outside of my office only a month ago. I'll bet he had something to do with this bullshit, anyway."

I looked at Walters. "You knew Earl Teller. You were doing business with the National Brotherhood."

Walters added more whiskey to his glass. His hand was getting shakier. He kept his head down, eyes away from me.

Simms rested a hand on Rachel Walters' shoulder. "Let Carl take you to get lunch, then go to the station while we sort through some things. Get away from here."

She shook her head. "I'm staying with Dickie."

"For fuck's sake, Rachel, just go already," Walters said. "He's ready to fuck you where you're sitting, and I'm not in the mood to watch."

Simms put an arm around her and leaned in and whispered in her ear. She listened, nodded, stood, and walked over next to Carl. "I guess I'm all yours, big man," she said, mustering up a smile.

Thompson returned the smile. He looked human, and not like the shaved gorilla/Rottweiler hybrid he usually looked like. "My pleasure," he said. He extended an arm, and she took it and they walked out together.

Simms crossed the room and shut the door and turned the lock. The sound of the bolt clicking echoed.

To Simms, I said, "Can I hit him?"

Simms shrugged. "I don't even know what you're talking about."

Walters didn't have time to respond. By the time I reached him and he realized what was about to happen, he had set his glass down and raised his left arm in defense.

I caught him with a right cross that left his eyes blank and him rolling onto his heels and hitting the built-in bookshelf behind him and sliding to the floor. His head slumped forward and a trickle of blood and drool dribbled from a corner of his mouth.

I gave him a backhanded bitch slap across his face. His back pressed against the shelf, and he struggled to drag himself away from me.

"Sheriff!" he said.

Simms perused the bookshelves on the other side of the room with Woody. Woody pulled a book and showed it to Simms.

"Haven't read it," Simms said. "Any good?"

"Very," Woody said.

I grabbed Walters and pulled him to his feet and shoved my left hand into his face. "You see this? Those Nazi assholes did this." I let go of him and he relaxed. I drove my right fist into the stomach. He doubled over, and I pounded him upside the head. He screamed and grabbed the back of his skull. I pulled him upright and got close enough to him I could smell every drink he'd consumed that morning. "They cut off my goddamn finger because I got involved with your stupid ass."

Simms froze and stared at me. "He lost his finger?" he said. He sounded shocked because, well, who wouldn't, you hear shit like that?

"Yeah," Woody said. He was still looking over the library. "Nasty shit. What do you think of Flannery O'Connor?"

I took Walters by the hair. I might have accidentally on purpose thumped his head against the bookshelf. A Stephen King tome came loose and fell on his head. It was one you could use as a doorstop, and it landed with a thud across the top of his skull. He gave a pitiful yell. I knocked his head across the books again.

"I didn't 'lose' a finger," I said. "It didn't fucking fall off." I flicked at the inside of Walters' eye, and he jumped a little, and I knocked his head into the shelf again. "My finger was fucking cut off by the assholes you work with. You opted to fuck the high priestess of racist asshole crackers, and it has dragged you into a meth operation, money laundering, gun running—"

From across the room, Simms said, "He did what the fuck?"

I looked over my shoulder at Simms, held a good grip on Walters, and said, "The counselor here helped the Brotherhood launder millions in meth money they're using to buy guns so they can start a race war. Compound that with the Brotherhood's belief that Bobbi Fisher stole three hundred thousand of those dollars, which you and I both know is high-grade bullshit since you stole it."

Simms walked around the peripheral of the room and moved into my line of sight. It was difficult to focus on much that wasn't Walters at that point.

"That changes shit," Simms said. "You're talking about federal-level crimes. We need the Feds on this."

"Awesome," I said. I kicked Walters in the stomach. He grunted and balled his body up, as if he could vanish into nothingness.

"Stop fucking hitting me. Please." Walters' words came out as wet little sobs.

"Have they moved Teller's car yet?" I said to Simms.

"No," he said. There was a measure of caution in his voice. "Why?"

I took hold of Walters and pushed him toward the door. Simms stepped in front of me.

"Where are you taking him?" he said.

"He needs fresh air," I said, bum-rushing past him.

Walters relaxed his body into dead weight. I braced myself to keep him standing, grabbed him with both hands, and kept moving toward the front door, using momentum to propel him forward. He screamed something about suing the county and the sheriff's department and me and anyone else he could think of. That was when his head brushed against the door frame hard enough to make a crack, and he yelled about that instead.

The outside air was crisp and harsh. As I brought Walters down the front porch steps he decided his crotch hitting each step wasn't what he wanted, so he gave up on passive resistance and pushed himself to his feet.

The deputies and state troopers looked at us with confused expressions. Simms was on the porch and yelled, "Stand down, guys! Stand down!"

I shoved Walters toward the open trunk of Teller's burned-out wreck and held him there. Teller's body looked worse than it had the night before. Bits of charred flesh clung to bone burned black. The heat from the fire had scorched clothing straight onto the skeleton, leaving rags hanging from his ribcage. The smell was a combination of burned flesh and rotten meat and piss, the stench shoving itself into the recesses of your nostrils, finding a place to burrow in deep and not give up.

"That was Earl Teller," I said. "He made the mistake of telling me the Brotherhood's business, so they doused him in gas and set him on fire, and once he was done burning to death, they pissed on his smoldering corpse. Want to guess who had front-row seats to that Rob Zombie nightmare right before they chopped his finger off? I'll save you the effort; it was me, motherfucker. Do you even give a good goddamn why? They were proving a point." I pushed his head down until his face was almost pressed against the remains of Earl Teller. "The point was they want their goddamn money."

Walters flailed and screamed and broke free from me. He trembled, covered in sweat, his eyes wide and wild. "Goddammit, I didn't take the money, I swear to fuckin' Christ, I didn't—" He tripped over his own feet and landed on his ass. "They asked me where the money was and I said I didn't know. That's the honest to God truth, I swear on my fucking life."

Simms watched from the edge of the driveway. The deputies stood behind him, waiting to be told what to do, clueless as hell in the meanwhile.

"What the hell happened, Malone?" Simms said.

I told him about the meth house and Monica Mayhew in bullet points. As I talked, his expression would change to a new level of disbelief, and he'd run his hand through his hair and shake his head and mutter an obscenity and then tell me to keep talking.

"Why am I just finding out Bobbi Fisher is alive?" he said. "Biggest news in this county in months, and she shows back up on your doorstep and you don't think to tell anyone?"

Dickie—or Richie, or whatever the fuck people wanted to call him—had passed out in the driveway. None of the deputies bothered to move him. He snored next to a burned-out wreck with well-done human remains in the trunk.

Simms' radio burst to life. "Ten-double zero, ten-double zero!" a voice said. "Officer down! Officer down!"

Simms snapped the radio off his belt. "This is Sheriff Simms. Report."

It was Thompson. "There was an ambush, Matt! They shot me, and they got Rachel!"

Simms told a deputy to stay at Walters' house while the rest of the deputies and state police officers headed to the hospital. He had us drag Walters back into the house and handcuff him somewhere so he couldn't get anywhere. Walters was unconscious the entire time, so we didn't worry about being gentle. Woody said the bathroom seemed the most merciful place, since he was likely to have to piss or puke when he woke up, so we cuffed him to the pipes under the sink, then followed Simms.

Woody drove. I tapped the fingers I had left on the dashboard. I thought of sitting in a thunderstorm, in a pool of my own blood on the side of the highway, and the rush of mortality that

181

overwhelms you. It's the fucking cliched realization that all it takes is one person, one second, the wrong place, the wrong time, and it all changes...

Woody's cell phone rang. He fished it from his pocket and answered.

"Hello? Hey...wait, wait, calm down. Take a deep breath. What's wrong? What did he say?" There was a long pause. "Fuck. No. We're on the way to the hospital, and then we'll be there. Do not go anywhere. I know. I know. But stay where you are. No, we're both fine. But you need to stay right where you are. Promise me. Promise me this, Bobbi. I'll call you once things settle. Henry and I, we'll take care of this. It'll be okay."

Woody hung up the phone. "Mitch Fisher called Bobbi. Someone grabbed her girls at school."

CHAPTER 36

Simms was in the Parker County General ER waiting area when we walked in, drinking coffee from a paper cup and staring at his shoes like there were answers to the question of life on them.

"How's he doing?" I said.

"He's alive," Simms said. "Two shots to the chest area, but he was conscious when they brought him in. He's in surgery now."

Simms had stayed on the radio with Thompson until paramedics showed up. It went down outside the sheriff's department as Thompson had pulled into his spot and had gone around to open the door for Rachel. A pickup pulled up and two men in masks and carrying AR-15s jumped out. Thompson pulled his service weapon and opened fire as he tried to push Rachel back into the car, but the driver swung the semi-auto around and fired off half a clip. Several rounds nailed Thompson in the chest and he collapsed onto the sidewalk. Rachel screamed for Thompson, and then for Simms, as they shoved her into the pickup and drove away.

"Somehow, this whole thing managed to become fuckered up," Simms said.

That was when we told him about Bobbi and her daughters. He screamed and threw the paper cup across the waiting area, splattering coffee across the wall. The nurses stopped what they were doing and stared as Simms glowered and stormed out of the waiting area.

We found him outside, standing next to a sign that proclaimed the hospital a "smoke-free zone." Woody handed him a pack of cigarettes and a lighter. Simms lit up and sucked in smoke. He jabbed in my direction with the burning cigarette.

"Just to give you the heads up, in this moment, I hate you." He turned to Woody. "And I'm not sure what to make of you."

"I'm the guy who gave you a cigarette," Woody said.

I said, "Listen, Sheriff, I know—"

"The fuck you know, Malone," Simms said. "My best friend's gutted open on a surgical table, and now there's two little girls and my ex-wife grabbed by a bunch of goddamn psychopaths. All this shit does is wind back to your narrow ass, so I'm not sure I care what you think know, 'cause the life of everyone you come into contact with goes to shit in seconds." He sucked down another drag. "Witnesses at the courthouse gave us an ID on the pickup, so the state police are starting a search."

I lit a cigarette. "You know like I do where they are."

Simms rubbed his hand across his face. "The state boys are talking about mobilizing the National Guard, and the FBI bringing in a tactical unit."

"Jesus Christ but that's a shit-storm of bad ideas in just one sentence."

"I told them the last thing they need is to bust into that compound. Not a soul in there would blink at killing a cop, and they'll all fight to the death if the Mayhews tell them to." Simms lit a fresh cigarette, took a deep inhale, blew out a stream of smoke.

In the distance there was the cry of an ambulance, growing stronger as it drew closer. No one's life got better at either end of a siren, and once the sound had faded to memory, there would be loss to unpack, tears to be shed, pain to salve.

At least Doria was safe. That's the definition of being a selfish asshole, was concern about the woman peripheral to your life while those around you struggled to cope with their hurt.

Fuck.

Doria.

I called her number on my cell and waited, air caught in my throat. I walked off, away from Simms.

The phone rang. I paced. One. Two. Three. Four. Tension twisted in my gut.

On five, there was an answer.

"Hello," she said. Her tone was even, practiced, almost unnatural. "Henry?"

"Hey. I was checking—"

"Henry," she said again. This time, there was a quiver in her voice.

I swallowed. "Yes?"

"Someone wants to speak to you."

There was a pause, and another voice said, "Mr. Malone. I trust we have your attention."

It was Monica Mayhew.

"You do," I said.

"Wonderful. Here are your instructions, and you'll follow them to the letter, or people die. You will get my money from whoever has it, and you'll deliver it in two hours. If not, I'll kill someone. After that, you'll have thirty minutes to get the money, at which point I'll kill someone else. Another thirty minutes, someone else dies. You can do the math here. And to make it more interesting for you, there won't be bodies to bury. Try to involve the police, everyone dies. None of this is negotiable."

Somewhere inside me, there were words, but they weren't going anywhere.

"Mr. Malone," Monica Mayhew said. "Are you still with me?"

"I'm here."

"Are we clear then?"

"Crystalline."

"Wonderful. I'll be calling in ninety minutes with instructions."

The line fell dead.

Simms was leaning against the wall, still smoking. When he

saw me, he said, "What's up?"

"We've got to get back to Walters' house."

"I can't. The state police want to talk to me in twenty minutes about—"

"Fuck the state police," I said "I just got off the phone with Monica Mayhew. She's holding onto everyone, and she's threatening to kill them starting in two hours if we don't deliver that money to her."

Simms' shoulders dropped like someone had tied anvils to them.

"Goddammit."

Woody took his truck to pick up Bobbi, and Simms and I drove back to Walters' house. Two deputies stood in the driveway. They seemed surprised when Simms charged from his car, pointing to the empty spot in the driveway where Teller's car had been.

"Where'd the car go?" Simms said.

A deputy, a skinny kid not old enough to shave, said, "State guys hauled it away."

Simms ran toward the front door as the deputy yelled after him, "How's Carl?"

Once I got inside, I heard the scream from upstairs, followed by smacks and another scream. I walked in as Simms kicked Walters in the gut and Walters tried to dance out of the way. He was still handcuffed to the pipe underneath the sink, and he spun and squirmed like a fish on a hook, knowing there wasn't anywhere for him to go.

I grabbed Simms and pulled him back. He kicked at empty space and tried to squirm away from me. His breathing was hard and strained, his face red.

I held tight to Simms' shoulder. "We need him for now. We get everyone back, I'll help you beat the shit out of him."

Simms stopped and stood there breathing hard. He nodded

and handed me a set of keys and walked out of the room.

Walters' eyes were four shades of bloodshot, his face lumpy as bad mashed potatoes and bruised purple as a sunset. There was fresh blood from a new cut along his left cheekbone. A chunk of Walters' hurt was on me, and Simms batted clean up after it. Neither of us would lose sleep over that.

I unlocked Walters' handcuff from the sink pipe, dragged him into the shower, and turned the cold on full-blast. Rivets of ass-kicking poured down on him. He screamed like a scalded cat. After a minute I pulled him out. With his hair soaked and blanketed into his eyes, he looked more pathetic than he had. His teeth chattered, then stopped, and he opened his mouth and a tooth dropped out and rolled around the inside of the tub, rattling against the porcelain like a roulette ball on the wheel.

"You awake?" I said.

He nodded and shivered.

"Good, because you didn't have another fucking choice." I pulled him toward the bathroom door. "There's shit to do."

CHAPTER 37

I made a pot of coffee and planted Walters in a chair in the kitchen and handed him a cup. He sipped and made a face.

"Can I get sugar or something in this?" he said. The tooth he'd spit out was a canine, so he whistled a little when he spoke.

Outside the kitchen doorway, Simms paced back and forth like an expectant father in the 1950s. He was on the phone with the state police, trying to talk them up while not saying anything, either. He stopped and looked in and glared at Walters. Walters shrunk up like a dog smacked with a newspaper and drank more coffee.

I made myself a cup and drank some. It was terrible, but I didn't care. I wanted a drink of something else, but pushed the idea away and swallowed another gulp of coffee.

I hated not doing anything. Not that there was much I could do. I realized I had one card to play, and I called Jackie Hall. He wasn't thrilled to hear from me.

"You couldn't call at a shittier time," he said. There was the gentle roar of activity in his background, lots of voices, orders being given, vehicles moving, everything sounding busy and official.

"Timing has always been my gift, Jackie."

"I suspect you're only calling because you need something, and I can guess what it's about. Dare I ask how deep into this shit storm you are?"

I told him about the phone call from Monica Mayhew.

"Goddammit, Henry." He sounded pained and mournful. "You need to get over here. The Feds find out about this, they will want to talk to you."

"I can't, Jackie. I need you to buy us some time."

"'Us'? There's an 'us?' Who the fuck is your 'us'? Whatever you're considering, Henry, I'm gonna beg you to not. This is big. You need to stand the fuck down and let professionals handle this."

"They'll kill them, Jackie. They'll murder those little girls."

Jackie sucked in a quantity of air that would have depressurized airplanes. "When this was nothing but drugs and rednecks, I told you it was bigger than you. That shit was microscopic compared to the scale of now. The Feds set up a command post, they're bringing in negotiators and strategists and want to storm the compound. It's a goddamn action movie here. You do not know what the fuck you're doing or appreciate the gravity of what you're dealing with."

"How long before the Feds do anything."

"I can't say. A few hours, max."

"Thank you, Jackie."

"Henry—"

I cut off the call.

Simms came into the kitchen as I hung up my phone. "Who you jawing with?"

"Jackie Hall."

"What's that fat-ass got to say?"

"He sends his love. The Feds won't go Michael Bay on shit before our clock runs out with Monica Mayhew."

"Perfect." He turned to Walters. "Which gives you an excellent opportunity to tell us where the money is."

Walters slurped down the last of his coffee. "I don't know, goddammit. Why the fuck would I keep lying to you about it if I did?"

"Your lips are moving, Dickie, so I assume you're lying,"

Simms said. "It might be easier to believe you except our history together is a bit rough."

Walters tried to stand up, and realized too late that was a shitty idea, and collapsed into a pile on the floor. He pushed himself up and leaned back.

"Christ, Sheriff. When are you just going to face up to the fact you were a shitball of a husband married to his job, and didn't give her time, and I did, instead of keeping a hard-on over the fact I'm with her and you're not."

Simms dropped his head low and stared at Walters. "It's more to do with you being a lying sack of mule shit, Dickie. Plus, you fuck around on her like it's a full-time job and you were stupid enough to get neck-deep into a meth-and-gun operation, and there are people in danger who have done nothing to deserve this," Simms said. "It's less about you being a philandering fuckwad and more to do with you being a general issue gob of dick snot. So again I ask, where is the money?"

"And again, I say, I don't know," Walters said. The pain and shame of the beatdowns was wearing off, and he was trying to take back the vibe of the in-control lawyer. That was hard to do when you were missing teeth. Now he looked like a gap-toothed idiot in pricey silk slacks. "Fucking Bobbi took it right before she up and vanished. I haven't seen it since she left."

I poured myself more coffee. "Back to you being dick snot for a minute. How'd jacking neo-Nazi drug money seem like a good idea, anyway?"

Walters shrugged. "This system they've got set up, they run shit through West Virginia, Ohio, Virginia, Kentucky, some states down south. They're hooked up with biker gangs and these other white power groups, the real fucking deal, nasty-ass motherfuckers, and they couldn't make the shit fast enough to keep up with demand. The Brotherhood, they kept asking me to do more, and they weren't going to just let me walk away clean, and I needed an escape plan. They were funneling so much money to off-shore accounts and then buying shit and using me as the in-between, it wasn't hard to take a few bucks here and there."

"Which came out to three hundred grand?" Simms said.

"It could have been more than a few bucks here and there, then."

"Goddamn cocky for you to think they wouldn't notice your hands in their pockets," I said. "People notice when the cash drawer is light."

"We're not talking about Mensa members here. They're all lowlife mouth-breathers. There's not a forensic accountant in that bunch."

"The mouth-breathers figured it out," Simms said.

"And Bobbi?" I said. "Was she part of your getaway plan?"

Walters laughed. "Right. Because you take the garbage with you when you go on vacation. That cunt was disposable."

Simms gave Walters a hard look. "And Rachel?"

Walters looked away from Simms. It was as if someone had caught him with his dick in a vacuum cleaner. Shame wasn't a thing he had much experience with.

Simms nodded. "I'll give you the courtesy of not making you lie about that, then."

"What about the money?" I said. "Where was it when it vanished?"

"Upstairs, in a suitcase in the master bedroom. It was ready to go. Hundred-dollar bills, non-sequential. I..." He shook his head. "I fucking had this. That's why it's got to be Bobbi. She had to have taken it."

That was when I had one of those "moments of clarity" we talk about in AA, where shit comes together and makes sense.

I said, "Mayhew didn't take them back to the compound."

"What do you mean?" Simms said.

"Mayhew's crazy, but she's not stupid. Hostages are an insurance policy. She's needs them safe, away from violence."

Simms chewed on his lip. "What if she's counting on violence, though?"

"She is, but from the government. She's expecting an attack the compound, and she knows that regardless of whatever training they have, they don't have the firepower to take on a full assault, but they won't back down, either. They'll fight to the last man because of her."

"It'll be Ruby Ridge all over again, on a twenty-four-hour news cycle, perfect to stir up the cause. Combine it with what you told me about the guns, and she's setting up a tidal wave of violence. So she had all of this planned."

"Doubtful. Luck, synchronicity, and Walters being an idiot converged at the right moment, and she's working with the moments she's got. There may have been a master plan, but she's veered from that and she's winging it now."

"Which means she's willing to take bigger risks." Simms' body went slack, and he slumped against the wall. "We're fucked, aren't we?"

"Right up the ass."

CHAPTER 38

Simms and I were outside smoking when Woody's truck pulled up and he and Bobbi got out. Simms took a last drag off of his cigarette and crushed it underneath his foot.

"For all the pictures I've seen of her, I somehow expected her to look different," he said.

"How so?" I said.

"I'm not sure. She's raised a certain amount of chaos. You want the eye of the storm to be something, I suppose."

Woody nodded at us as they approached. Bobbi kept close to his side, hands twisted together. Tears had taken off most of her makeup, and half-hearted efforts to reapply it weren't successful. All you saw was pain, worry, and flushed cheeks.

"Where's Walters?" Woody said.

"He's handcuffed back inside," Simms said. He looked at Bobbi. "It's nice to finally meet you face to face, Ms. Fisher, though I wish you'd told us before now you weren't dead."

Woody took a protective step in front of Bobbi. "Her girls are gone, Sheriff. Let's get what matters out of the way first, then we'll deal with the other shit."

"Agreed."

I finished my cigarette. "Come on, Bobbi. I'm sure Dickie will be thrilled to see you again."

Walters had balked at us handcuffing him back into the bathroom. Simms had worked around that by threatening to beat
him senseless with the butt of his gun. Walters had acquiesced
without much fuss.

When Bobbi Fisher came into Walters' view, he went ape shit
and tried to pull free and called Bobbi a lot of things that would
have shamed his mother.

Woody's fists clinched and his eyes cool and steady. He was
a snake, waiting to strike.

Simms walked into the bathroom and slapped Walters.
Walters froze and stared at Simms like a frightened animal.

"I'll take those cuffs off," Simms said. "You do anything
stupid, meaning anything you'd normally think is smart—" He
pointed to Woody. "And I'll let him get a hold of you and do
whatever he wants to do to you. So can you behave?"

Walters didn't move for a beat. His head moved slightly. A
nod. "Yes."

Simms unlocked the cuffs and Walters walked into the bedroom, rubbing his wrists, Simms a step behind him, his hand
resting on top of his gun.

Woody and Bobbi sat on the edge of the bed. Bobbi cried
quietly into her hands. Woody kept an arm around her shoulders.

Walters said, "There any chance I can get a drink?"

"No, there's not," I said, and pointed to a chair on the far
side of the room. "Sit your ass down now."

Walters did as told. He had pushed whatever luck he had as
far as it could go.

Simms said, "I'm fresh out of brilliant ideas right now.
They're expecting their money." He threw glances toward
Walters, then Bobbi. "Neither of you want to admit you've got
it, and you don't seem to care that there are lives at risk here."

Bobbi cried louder. She pulled her face up and wiped tears
from her eyes.

"Why don't we call the state police or the Feds and tell them
what's happening?" she said.

"Because Monica Mayhew has gone off the reservation on this one," I said. "She's decided she's got nothing to lose, and she won't blink at killing people."

My cell phone rang. It was Doria's number.

I felt everyone staring at me. I stared at the phone as it continued to ring.

Simms said, "Answer it. I'm sure the crazy bitch has plenty to say."

I swallowed hard and answered. "Hello."

"Mr. Malone," Monica Mayhew said. "You have my money?"

I had no clue what to do in that moment. We didn't have a plan, or even options. All we had was the hope she wouldn't start killing people we cared about. So I gave her the only answer I could.

"I do," I said.

"Wonderful. Here's what I need you—"

"But I want to speak to Doria."

She laughed. "Don't you have the big balls, making demands."

"I want to know she's okay."

"Do you think you have some kind of power or authority, Mr. Malone?"

"I think I've got your three hundred grand, which should buy me two minutes on the phone." I softened my voice. "Let me know she's alive, everyone else is fine. Throw me that fucking bone, Mayhew."

There was a pause. Maybe it was only a second or two, but it felt like a goddamn eternity. Things got quiet, there were deadened voices in the background, then Doria said, "Henry?"

"It's me. How are you?"

"I'm great, Henry. Never fucking better."

"What about the girls?" I said.

"They're scared, but they're fine. Rachel and I, we're trying to keep them calm, telling them they'll be home soon. Tell Bobbi she can expect big therapy bills someday."

"How are you and Rachel?"

"We're terrified. Probably more than the girls are." She laughed. "These two are out of their minds, if you hadn't figured it out. And they're fucking shitty hosts, too." There was a noise like a body blow, and Doria grunted.

I cringed. Everyone in the room stared at me with fear, apprehension, wondering what I'd heard. I waved my hand, trying to convey "Everything's good." It was a lie, but lies were what I had at the moment.

Things were quiet again and Monica Mayhew got back on the phone. "Are we pleased?"

"Yeah, we're goddamn awesome."

"I'm so thrilled you're happy. Nothing brings me greater pleasure."

I worked to keep a rising stream of anger from erupting. I gritted my teeth and my hand tightened around the phone.

"You know the Feds are ready to storm the compound," I said. "You have no issue in letting the government kill your own people?"

"That action will be on a group of peaceful individuals defending themselves against the ire of an illegitimate government," she said. "It will be beautiful to watch the media play it out for weeks on end. It will feed that resentment, that frustration, there underneath the surface and waiting for the slightest provocation. There will be righteous action, as white citizens rise up, timed as we flood the cities with weapons, and crime goes rampant. This nation will take arms against the mongrel hordes, and all right-minded white people will see the ignorance of allowing the purity of our race to be erased. We will wash clean the niggers, the queers, the feminists, the spics, the Muslims, all the people who would turn us into some big brown stew of homogeneousness, and wipe the white race out from the nation we founded."

Monica Mayhew was, without a doubt, so far out of her goddamn mind that reality was a fairy tale she heard as a bedtime story at night. She very well could get the money and still kill everyone. She might just do it as a point of amusement.

"Where do you want me to bring the money?" I said.

She named a restaurant in town, a mom-and-pop diner where miners and families came in to eat. It was always busy.

"Be there in an hour," she said.

The line fell dead.

I shoved the phone in my pocket. Different faces looked up at me, expressions varying from curiosity to apprehension to fear.

I turned to Simms. "I need you to make calls and make them quickly."

CHAPTER 39

The Riverside Cafe had been there as long as anyone could remember, on the corner across from Walgreen's and down the street from the hotel where railroaders stayed between trains. The booths were all original, and the vinyl had the cracks and duct tape repairs to prove it. In no small amount of irony, the Riverside Cafe was three blocks from the river.

The crowd was sparse, shoveling away orders of fried eggs and bacon. A waitress moved table to table filling coffee cups. The old man at the register beside the door whistled and read the newspaper.

I sat in a booth in a corner furthest from the door, with a gym bag next to me. I tapped the fingers I had left across the linoleum tabletop and checked the door every five seconds.

My left hand ached. It hadn't been more than eight hours since I'd woken up and found out what had happened. That morning seemed a lifetime ago. I wondered how Jack Bauer made it through a day.

The bell over the door jingled and Jeremiah Mayhew walked in. The old man at the register said something to him, and he brushed him off, caught sight of me, and walked to my booth, sliding into the seat across from me.

"Mr. Malone. Long time, no see. It seems you were unable to learn a simple lesson and to stay out of the business of others." He glanced at my hand. "How it that?"

I raised my hand. "Barely notice it now."

"What a shame. Certain losses should linger, so they are appreciated, and you understand what ignorance cost you." His eyes drifted over to the duffle bag. "That the money?"

I moved my hand on top of the bag. "It is."

"Mind opening it up for me?"

"In fact, I do."

The waitress came up to the table. The coffee pot was half full, steam rising from inside. She refilled my cup.

"Get you anything, honey?" she said, twisting toward him. She jerked awkwardly as she moved and the coffee pot came loose from her hands and flipped through the air. Coffee flew from the pot and splattered across him.

He screamed and jumped, his knees ramming into the table. He glared at the waitress and brought his arm back, fist ready.

My right hand dived into the gym bag and came back out with a nine-millimeter pistol. I leveled it at his chest. He stopped screaming and dropped the fist. His eyes focused on the pistol.

"What are you doing?" he said.

"I'm taking my own hostage," I said. "Or I might shoot you because I want to. Could go either way."

He shook his head in that slow, deliberate manner that meant he thought I was full of shit. "We're in a restaurant full of people. Even you aren't that kind of stupid."

There was the sound of the hammer on a pistol being cocked. Jeremiah Mayhew cranked his head to the side. The waitress had taken a shooter's stance, pistol in hand and aimed straight at his head. Every other noise in the restaurant dropped and the only sound was each person breathing.

I leaned in closer across the table. "Jeremiah, buddy, you don't know what kind of stupid I am."

"You're marking a very poor life choice."

"Won't be the first one, and sure as hell won't be the last. But the way I figure it, you should be worth something to Monica Mayhew."

His mouth flickered into a grin. "She won't give them up for me. My sister is far too determined to cave to that simple of demands."

"Is that the thing you want to bet the farm on? Because I suspect the reason she sent you is because she wouldn't trust anyone else but her own flesh and blood with the cash. That in mind, I'm also confident she'd prefer you're alive."

Jeremiah Mayhew must have figured I'd already pieced it all together. Maybe he thought it was common knowledge. For whatever reason, he didn't respond. He seemed more concerned about the waitress with a gun in his face. She was a wisp of a thing, and you would have thought the weight of the pistol would topple her over. She looked more comfortable holding the gun than she had the pot of coffee.

Mayhew's eyes shifted between her and me. "Why the fuck is this bitch holding a gun on me?"

"I'd watch your language. She's a sheriff's deputy, as is everyone else in here." I pointed to the register. "Except him. That's my dad."

At the register, Billy held a double-barreled shotgun he'd brought out from underneath the counter.

"You all aren't the only ones to drag family into this nonsense," I said.

Jeremiah Mayhew rested his palms flat on the table. He had an eerie stillness, his mouth flat and even, his breathing steady.

"What do you believe is going to happen next?" he said.

"That you'll take me to your sister."

"And if I tell you to fuck off instead?"

"Then I drive you somewhere and I put a bullet through the back of your skull."

His stare would have put holes in sheet metal. He kept it focused on me like laser beams. Nothing registered on his face. Fear, nervousness, anticipation. Absolutely nothing.

"She will kill them, you know," he said. "The women, the children, they will all die. This is a matter of principle to her.

How prepared are you to carry that with you for the rest of your life, however short it will likely be?"

"I guess the question for you is how prepared are you to be dead? She can kill me and those women and those kids, and you'll still dead, won't you?"

He shook his head. "You're threatening my life in front of a sheriff's deputy. You are a fresh kind of stupid."

The waitress leaned forward and pressed the barrel of her gun against the side of Jeremiah Mayhew's head.

His eyelids fluttered ever so slightly, and he swallowed hard.

I set my own pistol on the table. "If I don't kill you, someone else in here will. You put one of their own in the hospital, so you don't have friends in this place. If you feel the cause is worth dying for, we can make it happen. Plus, your sister doesn't get her money, and she kills four innocent people. Tough to rally around that. Don't look for a big uprising among your close-eyed kinsmen, since even they don't cotton to murdering women and children."

I patted the gym bag with my free hand. "Play the scenarios however you like. You won't get out of here alive unless it's with me next to you."

Jeremiah Mayhew nodded.

"Also, I wouldn't count on your sister's principles too much," I said. "She's using heroin, most likely in withdrawal, and no one makes good decisions at that point."

The corner of Jeremiah Mayhew's mouth twitched. "You don't understand shit about her or our plans."

"I understand neither of you are as fucking smart as you tell yourselves you are," I said. "If you're the hope for the white race, we might deserve to go extinct."

Simms came out of the kitchen as I led Jeremiah Mayhew through the diner. Simms saw him and punched him in the stomach. Mayhew doubled over, giving Simms the opportunity to kick him in the face. It shattered Mayhew's nose, and blood poured onto the floor before he could right himself.

I grabbed a bunch of paper towels from a table and handed them to Mayhew. He buried his face in them. He soaked them in red within seconds.

"Man's a bleeder," I said.

"Wouldn't haven't been worth it otherwise," Simms said.

The plan came about in the time it took to realize Monica Mayhew had hung up on me. We emptied the diner of customers and filled it with deputies in civilian clothing in an hour. Simms hadn't been thrilled using Billy in the plan, but we were out of bodies and needed someone at the door.

"Billy'll have a gun on him the whole time," I had said. "He'll be fine."

Those hadn't been comforting words to Simms, but he'd agreed to it. He knew we didn't have options or time to argue.

Once Jeremiah Mayhew finished bleeding everywhere, he gave us directions to an old house out by McClusky Lake. He sat in a booth, his face covered in dried blood.

"Can I at least see the money?" he said.

I shrugged. "Sure." I flipped the gym bag over and dumped the contents onto the floor. Socks and T-shirts tumbled out and scattered across the black-and-white tile.

"Goddammit," he said.

CHAPTER 40

"You don't look like you've ever suffered any debilitating head wounds," I said. "How did you end up buying into the ignorance your family sells?"

We were in Jeremiah Mayhew's truck, Mayhew driving and me with a gun aimed at his midsection. His wrists were cuffed to the steering wheel, just to help keep everything honest.

Jeremiah Mayhew drove an F-150 pickup scabbed in rust around the wheel rims. The shocks needed work, too, or else he intentionally hit every rut and pothole he could find, throwing us around the inside of the cab. Either way, we bumped our way up the old road headed to the lake house.

He kept his eyes on the road. It was getting dark, and the sky was deep violet in the distance. The only light available was off his headlights.

"You have issue with our cause?" he said.

"Don't try to lump me with you on some 'our cause' nonsense. You stand on your own there. I have issue with you selling this 'us versus them' bullshit, turning everyone into an enemy. I want to believe people are better than what you give them credit for."

"You underestimate the simmering rage in this country. It's out there, and everyone hides it behind the politeness they teach you on Sunday mornings, but it's waiting, Malone, there for the perfect moment. When that moment comes, you'll be amazed at the anger, the frustration in people." His head twisted to give me an assessing once-over. "The sodomites march in our streets and get to call themselves 'married,' and politicians pander to people who live in our country but don't even speak our language. You and I, we're forgotten in the equation, and we're the ones who made America great."

"First things first, you and I are nothing alike. Second thing second, neither one of us have done jack to make this country great. We won two lotteries—genetic and geographic—by being born here. We ride on the backs of others before us, and you act like we have something coming because we burn easy in the summer."

He gave a dismissive snort. "Tell me how our country is better now than it was, when everyone understood their place. There was a time when white men decided and controlled the destiny of our world. Now we're nothing but a nation full of bullshit and self-doubt. We stopped building our own future, and we became nothing but consumers. We decided that it was okay to let in every mongrel dog and stray animal off the street. We used to know occasionally you had to kill them, no matter how much it made the children cry. It was safer for the other animals, and the kids remembered who was in control."

He was goading me, wanting to prove a point, trying to get a response. I wanted to prove I was better than that. Not to him, but at least to myself.

"Keep the recruitment speech for the dropouts and the in-breds," I said.

"Nothing I say will change your mind, Malone, You're too far gone. You try to live in the same stinking lie everyone else tells themselves. It's why you said what you did in the restaurant, about Monica—"

"Check out her eyes," I said. "Check her skin. She may have liver damage. You won't find track marks on her arms, but I look between her toes, or behind her knees. And I get you want to believe she's above something so base, but isn't she risking an awful lot for three hundred thousand dollars? She's flushing away your entire drug network, initiating this bullshit race war plan, a cop could still die, she's holding four people at gun point—" I let my voice trail off. "What's the benefit here? You get three hundred grand Walters stole from you. Percentage wise, how does that compare to how much you've made, or how much you'll make?" I turned my attention out the window and gave some silence for effect. "Something's not right, Jeremiah. You know that."

Jeremiah Mayhew, for once, kept his mouth shut, only looking forward and driving.

In the headlights I saw the lake house. It was an old two-story that rested at the end of a gravel road. There was a grove of leafless trees to one side, fanning out until they reached the hillside. On the opposite side was McClusky Lake, the moonlight reflecting off of its water, paper-thin sheets of ice floating in the stillness.

About a hundred feet from the house, I had Jeremiah Mayhew stop the truck. "Keep the headlights on," I said as I got out and walked around.

There were lights on inside the house, and I saw movement through the windows. The light was dim, probably battery-powered lanterns. Jeremiah Mayhew told me the property had belonged to one of the Brotherhood's true believers, left to the group in his will a decade prior, but nothing had ever been made from it. The wood was gray, rotted and worn. The shutters hung onto the windows with something akin to prayer. The yard was the size of a postage stamp, nothing but mud and weeds. It was still better than my place.

I opened the driver's door and blared the truck horn. A window opened, and I made out a silhouette standing at it.

"Monica!" I said.

The silhouette moved, and another one took its place.

"Mr. Malone!" Monica Mayhew called out from the window.

"This wasn't our agreement. And it's 'Ms. Mayhew,' if you please!" She pulled someone close to her. I couldn't make out the shape, just the struggle. "Since you're violating the terms of our deal, who do you think I should kill first?"

I unlocked the cuffs attached to the steering wheel and used them to pull Jeremiah Mayhew out of the truck. I pressed the barrel into the side of his stomach. He grunted.

"I'm voting that I blow your brother away," I said. "How's that sound?"

The two shadowy figures vanished from the window. The front door opened and shapes exited and came into the moonlight. It was Doria, led by Monica Mayhew. Mayhew held a gun underneath Doria's chin. Their movements were awkward, Monica Mayhew a half-foot taller than Doria, a painful dance as Mayhew hunched over to keep the gun in position, her other arm wrapped around Doria.

"Stop right there," I said.

They did.

Everything was silent. The only sound was winter birds that didn't have sense enough to migrate, rustling branches of dead trees and singing midnight lullabies.

In the glow of the truck lights, I made out the image of Monica Mayhew's face. It was nothing but a fist full of anger and barely concealed fear. She lacked the charm and reserve she used for the talk shows. This was the skull beneath the skin, stripped of muscle and sinew and civilization. She tapped the gun barrel against Doria's face.

"Let him go or I will splatter this bitch's brains into the woods," she said.

Doria kept as good a facade of cool as I'd ever seen on a human while having a gun pointed at them. Better than I'd ever done. She seemed more annoyed than scared. The woman had brass cojones. If we survived this, I might have to ask her to marry me.

"No, you won't," I said.

"Is that a test you want me to take, Mr. Malone?" Monica Mayhew said. "I will kill her and I will have my men inside kill the others."

"No, you won't, Monica, because there aren't any other men." I dug my gun deeper into Jeremiah Mayhew's ribs. "It's just you and your brother here. Because this was always just about the three hundred grand."

I pulled Jeremiah Mayhew another step forward. He snarled at me. Monica Mayhew startled. Her gun hand trembled, and Doria dropped that steely resolve for a heartbeat to let the fear show, then she went back to hardcore mode.

"How much are you into your dealers?" I said. "Do you owe them the whole three hundred grand, or was the plan to pay them off and then disappear somewhere with what was left?"

I inched Jeremiah Mayhew closer, keeping the gun tight against him. Monica Mayhew held her ground steady.

"I've tried to figure out why you kept Walters alive, especially after watching you burn Teller, and all I can think is that all you want is the money. Your brother here, he's a true believer, but you grew tired of being the pretty face, always in front of the camera, knowing you'd never be the real power, and when you couldn't find other ways to bury pain anymore, you shoved a needle into your arm. But the more you used, the more you owed, and drug dealers only extend that line of credit so far. Did you find out blowjobs only pay off so much?"

Jeremiah Mayhew pulled at the cuffs. "My sister is a blood-sworn member of the National Brotherhood—"

"Shut up, Jeremiah," Monica Mayhew said.

Jeremiah looked at her as if he'd watched her kick his puppy. "He's lying, Monica. He wants us to turn us against one another." The timbre in his voice, you couldn't tell if he was trying to convince her or himself.

Monica Mayhew wrenched her arm tighter around Doria. "I said to shut up."

I looked at Jeremiah Mayhew. "Your big sister wanted out. I

bet she told you the money was for something else, a big plan she had, but you got played, didn't you?"

"The cause—" Jeremiah Mayhew said.

"What cause?" Monica Mayhew said. "The Brotherhood? We're a joke, Jeremiah. The only reason that compound exists still is because we've been selling meth to bikers. The world doesn't need us."

"Bullshit! The world will rise up around the Brotherhood—"

"Fuck the Brotherhood. I've lived with nothing but the Brotherhood my entire life, trying to justify it to the rest of the world, and you know what I realized? That it will never be mine. It's in the goddamn name—the fucking Brotherhood—and it would always be yours, and I'd be nothing but a set of tits to show off."

"How did you know Walters was stealing from you?" I said.

"He was the only one who wasn't blood-sworn." There was a twinge of laughter in her voice. "Everyone else, every step of the way, they're sworn to the Brotherhood. They believe in the cause. But when our totals didn't add up, and we traced back our steps, we saw it had to be Walters." She glanced over her shoulder, back at the house, then me. Nerves were kicking in. Maybe she needed a fix. Maybe she realized everything was falling apart. "I owe forty grand, give or take. The rest, I was buying into a deal that'll net about three million, and I can say 'fuck you' to all of this shit and go have a real goddamn life."

Jeremiah Mayhew looked at me. Moonlight glistened in his tears. You could see in his face all of his little racist dreams and beliefs shattering, collapsing and crumbling, in the moment.

"She said once the race war had begun, we'd use the money to start fresh. A better National Brotherhood. No more drugs, no more pandering, just our beliefs. Show people we were right."

"It's over, Jeremiah," I said. We took a step forward. "We can end this now."

"Stop right there," Monica Mayhew said. Her finger tightened on the trigger.

"You only have yourselves now, Monica. Let this go. In the phone call, Doria said 'these two.' Not 'them,' and not 'these people.' It was specific. 'These two.' Because you two fuck-nuts are it. You've abandoned the Brotherhood for this. Stop this now before anyone else gets hurt. Before anyone dies."

Monica Mayhew said, "I want the money, that's all, Malone. Just give it and everyone walks away."

"There's no money, Monica. It's gone. The Feds confiscated it. Walters is turning state's evidence. He'll tell them everything. The National Brotherhood is history. Everyone knows what a fraud you are. There's nowhere to go. Let her go."

I was talking, buying time on shaky credit. It was bullshit, but I was counting on paranoia to keep her from figuring that out.

Monica Mayhew's face tightened. She knew she was running out of cards to play. Her eyes narrowed and her shoulders tightened and she smiled.

"Then I guess I have to kill her," she said.

That was when the red dot appeared on the side of Monica Mayhew's head. Dust and snowflakes danced in the line of light that ran back into the trees.

Jeremiah Mayhew sucked in a gasp of air. Monica Mayhew's eyes swam to the side. That quiver she had on her pistol intensified.

"Goddammit, I'm fucking serious!" Monica Mayhew said through her teeth. "I'll fucking kill her." She looked toward the laser sight. "I want my money!"

My throat closed shut. My focus went to the gun underneath Doria's chin.

I didn't notice Jeremiah Mayhew shifting his body ever so slightly, his left foot hooking around my right ankle, and the sudden jerk. My feet slid out underneath me, my body flying into the air, and I landed with a hard thud on my back.

Jeremiah Mayhew broke out in a run toward his sister. I looked up into the hillside where Woody was positioned with his sniper rifle.

"Do it!" I yelled.

The red dot dropped from Monica's head to Doria's calf. There was a gunshot and Doria screamed and her body lurched forward out of Monica Mayhew's grasp and she clutched her wound and fell to the ground.

Monica Mayhew swung her body toward the hillside, moving her gun up and taking a firing stance. The dot moved again, and her chest exploded in a geyser of red, and she buckled under the force of the shot. There were two more cracks of thunder, more blood, and her gun flew from her hand and she stumbled backward. She landed on the cold ground and didn't move.

I rolled to my side, brought up my pistol, and fired. The shot caught Jeremiah Mayhew in the right thigh. It sent him first onto his knees, then chest-down into the ground.

I pushed myself up onto my hands and knees. My right knee throbbed from the fall. I forced myself to my feet.

Jeremiah Mayhew dragged himself toward his sister's pistol. He still had another ten feet to clear. I walked up beside him and fired a shot into the ground, six inches from him. He pulled back as dust and rocks flew into the air. He rolled onto his back and stared at me, hands raised in surrender.

"I give up," he said.

I aimed my gun in his face. I watched him sweat, watched him wonder if I would pull the trigger. I wondered about it myself. I hadn't gotten to shoot Monica Mayhew, but a part of me thought any Mayhew would do in this moment. Jeremiah Mayhew owed me for all those albums he had shattered. Oh, and for sister cutting off my goddamn finger.

I fired a shot just to the left. The bullet missed him by two inches. He screamed like a six-year-old on the playground, then realized he hadn't died, and started to cry.

"You're not worth it," I said. "None of you are."

I dropped my gun to the side and walked over and picked Monica's weapon off of the ground.

I limped my way to Doria. She sat up, holding her leg. I

crouched down beside her.

"Let me see," I said.

She gave me a stare that would have withered a plastic houseplant. "Fuck you."

"Let me look at your leg first, then foreplay."

I pulled her hands away from her calf. Her hands were sticky with blood. The wound looked clean, a nick on the back of the calf, a lot of blood and pain but nothing she wouldn't heal from. I took a handkerchief from my pocket and pressed it against the wound, then took off my flannel shirt and tied it around her calf to apply pressure.

I didn't hear Woody come down from the mountainside or walk up behind me. He was simply there, holding a sniper rifle.

"I radioed for Simms to bring in an ambulance," he said.

"Check on the girls in the house, will you?"

Woody walked away without a word.

I looked at Doria. She kept her face turned away from me.

"He fucking shot me," she said.

"That he did. May have saved your life."

She pursed her lips together. "Fucking shot me." She looked at me. "Knowing you is not worth this shit, Henry."

"So I understand."

CHAPTER 41

I gave Doria a few days after getting shot before I called; it only seemed fair. She didn't sound thrilled when she answered the phone.

"Before you say anything," she said, "understand that I can't do this."

"'Hello' to you as well."

"I'm serious as a heart attack, Henry. I don't want to see you."

"Where are you?"

"I'm home, and no, you can't come and see me."

"Why?"

"Because I don't want to see you."

"Can I ask why?"

"You got me shot, Henry."

"I didn't tell Woody to shoot you. And for that matter, he did it, not me. I thought he'd just shoot Monica Mayhew in the head."

"Monica Mayhew's chin was digging into the crown of my skull, Henry. That would have been a hell of a shot to make."

"Woody could have made it."

"He told me he did it to take me out of the equation. It was a cleaner shot with me out of the way."

"He watched *Speed* the week before."

"Right. Shoot the hostage." There was a small laugh.

"When did you talk to him?" I said.

"Yesterday. He called to apologize. He seemed to feel that the gentlemanly thing to do was to say 'I'm sorry for shooting you in the leg,' and Hallmark doesn't sell that kind of card."

"It's an under-served market, I bet."

There was a pause so quiet, I thought she might have hung up, before she said, "I'll be honest that it wasn't getting shot that made me decide I can't see you, which is not a statement I ever imagined I'd make. It was always going to be you disappearing at Christmas and then you only showed up again when you needed something. That was wrong, and I hope you're sober now, and I hope everything works out for you, Henry, but we're done."

The line went dead. I heaved a deep breath, hung my head, and stared at my feet, waiting for answers to arrive that never did.

I thought about calling Maggie. I needed someone to talk to. I decided against it, though. The last thing I needed was more heartbreak in one day.

Maggie did end up calling me the next day, and I let the message go to voicemail. She said she'd heard about the Mayhews, and my part in everything, and that she was proud of me, and that she loved me, and that she'd gotten the job in Philadelphia.

"As per usual, I shouldn't even be talking to you," Jackie Hall said.

"You'd miss me if I didn't come around," I said.

"You, and the clap, that's what I'd miss." Then he reached into the box of donuts I brought with me and snagged two maple-glazed beauties.

It was late March and we sat in Jackie's office as life bloomed again in Parker County. The last stretch of winter had dragged its ass along like a dog across a carpet, keeping everything cold and covered in snow until two weeks prior, when the weather broke and the sun melted everything away. Someone had planted daffodils in flower boxes around the state police outpost. It was lipstick on a pig, sure, but you had to appreciate the effort

Snow had been the only thing keeping my life peaceful up to that point. It was difficult for there to be an investigation into a series of suspicious activities when you couldn't get your car out of a parking lot because of three-foot snow drifts. But the state police and the FBI did come around to my door, asking me questions about why Simms and I had gone off on our own after the Brotherhood, and didn't bother to tell them what was going on.

I said the track record with large governmental organizations dealing with these types of things wasn't what anyone would call "sterling," and besides, I figured the NSA had been listening, anyway. No one was amused. Except me. I was laughing. Fuck 'em, I figured.

They hadn't been happy about Monica Mayhew dying, either, since she was a lynchpin in the whole investigation. I said I'd watched her set a man on fire and that she'd cut off one of my fingers, so I didn't give a shit what they made them happy; her being dead brought me an immense amount of satisfaction.

"How long is Simms going to be under investigation?" I said to Jackie.

"You asking for you, or you asking for Simms?" He chewed a large bite of donut and swallowed it with a drink of coffee.

I shrugged. "I'm nosy. I like to know things." Simms and I had talked a time or two since everything, but what with a federal investigation breathing down our necks, we felt it best we keep a respectable amount of distance.

According to the newspaper reports, the county commission wasn't pleased with the sheriff's actions, even if it meant four kidnap victims were returned safely, a money-laundering operation was shut down, and the Brotherhood compound had been seized by the federal government and would be bulldozed to the ground over the summer. The commission put Simms on suspended leave with pay.

Jackie licked glaze off of his fingers. "Officially, I can't tell you that. Unofficially, I can say he should be back on duty by the end of the month. You know how that deputy is doing?"

"The doctors aren't sure when he'll walk again. He's up in Morgantown, doing physical therapy. Most likely he'll be there for a while."

"You should go up, give him some words of encouragement. A 'there you go, sport,' that sort of shit."

"I'm sure he'd be thrilled to see me."

The Feds swooped in and whisked Walters away somewhere so he could turn state's evidence against the Brotherhood and organizations it worked with. The state bar was ready to disbar, and he would have time on his hands since no one not on a Federal payroll wanted anything to do with him.

Which was fine with the now ex-Mrs. Walters, Rachel, who filed for divorce two days after the incident at the lake house and moved back in with Simms. I was sure there was another reason I hadn't heard from Simms. Man probably didn't have time to breathe.

"How's the wife and kid?" I said.

"They're awesome. She's pregnant. Three months along."

"Pregnant during summer. That's fun."

"I'll go buy her ice cream when she asks."

That made me smile, because it was such an act of kindness and love, and because I didn't imagine it took much work to send Jackie to the frozen section at Kroger.

"You wanna come by sometime, have dinner?" Jackie said.

"Sure. She still a good cook?"

Jackie patted his stomach. "Do I look like I'm starving?"

Billy called up a little after six one evening, told me to hustle my ass up to his house. I reminded him gently that his son had a bum knee, and he could shove that hustle to a place sunshine would never know.

"Saddle that horse you call a dog and ride up here," he said. Once I got there, he motioned me into the living room and fiddled with the remote for his DVR.

"When d'you get a DVR?" I said.

"It's the twenty-first century, you old goat. Everyone's got DVR."

He rewound the six o'clock news and the blonde small-market anchor started out the broadcast with the announcement of the arrest of Wilson McGinley. They showed footage of McGinley, in a suit even worse than the one he'd been wearing the day I met him, being led out of the McGinley and Kurt offices by Federal marshals.

"Known throughout the state for his firm's television ads, McGinley was taken into custody today after federal prosecutors revealed he was suspected as a key member in the leadership of the National Brotherhood for the Advancement of European Heritage," she said. "Prosecutors said McGinley may be charged on as many as seventy different counts for his role in racketeering, money laundering, drug running, illegal arms deals, and murder."

The footage of Wilson McGinley coming out of the firm's offices in handcuffs, looking pissed as hell as he scowled and tried to hide his face as cameras flashed and reporters shoved microphones in his face, brought a smile to my face. It must have been the first time McGinley hadn't cheesed for the camera in decades.

"You aware of any of this?" Billy said.

"Nope," I said. "But I guess everything Walters has been telling the Feds led them there. It explains how Monica Mayhew chose Walters to set up the money laundering and the gun running, and why they cut him loose when things started to unravel."

"Figures. I ever tell you I know him? McGinley, I mean."

"I can't say it's come up in conversation."

"Graduated high school with him. He was a prick back then, too." He squinted at the TV. "Looks like he's had work done. Plastic surgery." He shook his head. "Fucking asshole." He turned off the TV. "I made spaghetti. You hungry?"

Izzy's tail whacked at the back of my knees at the mention of food. I rubbed her head.

"I could eat," I said.

CHAPTER 42

Bobbi Fisher called to tell me she was leaving Parker County and wanted to say goodbye. The whole world seemed to be moving forward without me.

Izzy and I were on the couch. I was following up on a movie recommendation from Woody, watching *The Friends of Eddie Coyle*, with Robert Mitchum getting pulled in deeper and deeper and struggling harder and harder to get out. But it was Mitchum, so the struggle looked relaxed and cool. He pulled that shit off better than I did.

She asked to meet me before she left, and she suggested the Walmart parking lot. This wouldn't be a lengthy farewell; she was a woman on a mission.

She drove a Toyota station wagon with a tag-along hooked to the back. Her daughters were in the back seat, each of them staring intently at electronic tablets. I pulled up next to her, and we each got out and leaned against the driver side bumper.

She looked better than when we'd first met. She had put back on some weight, filling her face out and adding color to her cheeks. Her hair was blonde and professionally done, with all of those highlights and lowlights that hairdressers always brag about. She wore a hoodie and skinny jeans and biker boots.

I motioned toward the expanse of cars in the parking lot and the greater expanse of nothing beyond the lot. "I'm stunned you're ready to leave all of this."

"It's time. The government can find me easy enough. They cleared me, so I figure I should get out of Parker County. Me and the girls need a change of scenery. Somewhere where everyone doesn't chat up every fucking detail of my life."

"Fresh air will do you a world of good," I said as I lit a cigarette, blissfully awash in my irony. "Where you headed?"

"Back up to Cincinnati. A friend got a job lined up for me."

"So much for the fresh air. Wish you the best. Shame we met under these circumstances. What about Woody? Are you and he still—"

"No. We said our goodbyes a few days ago. He's great, but he isn't really built for life with kids. Anyway, he'd just as soon die as leave here." She smiled at me. "I owe you a lot of thanks, Henry. What you did was fucking insane, and I'd have called anyone else a goddamn idiot for trying it, but you got my girls home and I can't imagine how to repay that."

I took a long drag off of my cigarette. "A share of that three hundred thousand would be nice."

She paused for a moment. Twisted her face up. Then she let it go. A smile returned to her face. "The Feds keep asking me about it."

"They still talking like Walters has it hidden somewhere?"

"No idea. Don't care, either. I'm not going out to buy a boat or nothing with it. That money will buy me and my girls a new life."

"It's dirty money, Bobbi."

"It won't be once I'm done with it."

I finished my cigarette and flicked it away. I wondered if I looked as cool as Mitchum. Not a chance in hell.

"Where's it been?" I said.

"In Cincinnati, hidden somewhere safe. That day the guys from the Brotherhood showed up at his house, I was nosing around in the closet and I found the suitcase and the money. When I figured out what Richie was into, with the Brotherhood, I used the spare key he gave me, snuck into the house when no one was there, and took the money."

"When did you and Jeremiah Mayhew hook up? Did he already know about the money, or did you tell him about it?"

She ran her hand through her hair and gave it all a good shake. "There's just no fucking secrets from you, is there, Henry?" She sighed. "When did you figure that part out?"

"When Walters kept telling me he hadn't sent Mayhew and Teller after me. I kept assuming that when they said to keep out of people's business, they were talking about Walters, but no, they were telling me to stay out of your business. Wasn't like there was a shortage of attention on you being missing, but the last thing needed was me adding to it."

She lit her own cigarette. "The stuff he believes isn't right, but he's not a bad guy, either. When he followed me after that day at Richie's house, I confronted him and, yeah, it's fucked up I slept with a guy stalking me, but I don't always make the sanest choices. When he and I figured out there was all this money, we talked out how to get away with it." She glanced back at her daughters. "I figure they'd blame Walters and kill him and that'd be the end. I'd come back and get the girls and Jeremiah would leave the Brotherhood and off we'd go."

"Except Monica Mayhew showed up and needed money to pay off a drug debt."

"She fucked everything up. Jeremiah said his loyalty was to his blood, so he picked that side of the fight."

"Which makes me wonder what you hoped for by stirring me into the pot, Bobbi. You showed up at my door thinking what?"

She turned away from me as if she had the capacity for shame or embarrassment. "Honestly?"

"No, Bobbi, lie like you have the entire fucking time. Goddammit, yes, tell me the goddamn truth."

She looked at me with a hard yet blank expression. "I hoped you'd kill them, and everything else would go away, and me and the girls, we could leave with the money."

I didn't even have words for that. It didn't keep me from

talking, though, because damn little ever does.

"That's maybe the worst fucking plan I've ever heard in my life. That is a plan so terrible, I'm shocked I didn't come up with it." I gestured toward the back seat of the station wagon. "What about them? You had the money. The Mayhews took your daughters. We could have bought time and gotten them the money and let this thing end."

"No. No. No." She repeated the word as if my suggestion was the craziest thing she'd ever heard. "They wouldn't have hurt my girls. They're—" She caught herself and she looked at her daughters for a long moment. "They're just little girls, Henry. Jeremiah wouldn't let her hurt them. Even with everything with his sister, they'd have been safe with him."

I remembered meeting Mitch Fisher, the catalyst for all of his, and his insistence on what a good mother his sister was. I wondered if he knew any of this, or if it mattered if he did.

Did she honestly believe all this? Even after everything that happened? After Teller? After me losing a finger? After Thompson getting shot and her daughters kidnapped? Was she really that convinced that the Brotherhood would have stopped at harming her daughters, that Jeremiah Mayhew was a man of his word?

She didn't give me the opportunity to ask those questions. She instead slung her arms around me and pressed her head against my chest. "We've got to hit the road." She pulled back and smiled at me. "Thanks again, Henry."

"Think nothing of it," I said as she got into the car and drove off. I suspected that she never would.

JAMES D.F. HANNAH is the Shamus Award-winning author of the Henry Malone novels, as well as the novel *The Righteous Path*. A native of eastern Kentucky and southern West Virginia, Hannah was an award-winning former journalist and columnist before moving into governmental public relations. He lives with entirely too many cats in Louisville, Kentucky.

BOOKS

On the following pages are a few
more great titles from the
Down & Out Books publishing family.

For a complete list of books and to
sign up for our newsletter,
go to DownAndOutBooks.com.

Final Cut
A Vince McNulty Thriller
Colin Campbell

Down & Out Books
December 2020
978-1-64396-155-2

Ex vice-cop Vince McNulty is technical advisor for Titanic Productions in Boston, but teaching Alfonse Bayard to walk like a cop is only part of McNulty's duties. At least it got McNulty to America, where he can search for his missing sister who was sold into adoption from Crag View Children's Home.

Investigating stolen film stock should have been a fairly innocuous task but when it leads to torture porn and snuff videos it soon turns into something much darker. And far more dangerous.

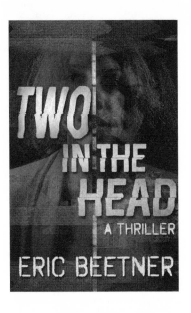

Two in the Head: A Thriller
Eric Beetner

Down & Out Books
January 2021
978-1-64396-170-5

Samantha Whelan is a DEA agent, and not always a straight and narrow one. She's been taking bribes and doing favors for Calder and Rizzo—big players in narco traffic in southern California—for years. She turned down a deal that night, but it meant killing her fiancé, an assistant district attorney. And it meant betraying her DEA brethren more deeply than she had so far. It was too much. So Calder and Rizzo tried to blow her up.

What happened then...she split. Samantha became Samantha and Sam. Two halves of the same person. The good side and the bad side. The two opposing forces living within her for so long were now free to fight it out to see who will win control.

All Due Respect 2020
Chris Rhatigan & David Nemeth, editors

All Due Respect, an imprint of
Down & Out Books
November 2020
978-1-64396-165-1

Twelve short stories from the top writers in crime fiction today.

Featuring the work of Stephen D. Rogers, Tom Leins, Michael Pool, Andrew Davie, Sharon Diane King, Preston Lang, Jay Butkowski, Steven Berry, Craig Francis Coates, Bobby Mathews, Michael Penncavage, and BV Lawson.

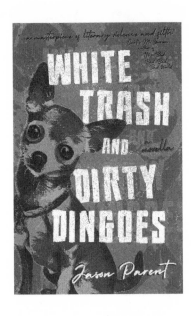

White Trash and Dirty Dingoes
Jason Parent

Shotgun Honey, an imprint of
Down & Out Books
July 2020
978-1-64396-101-9

Gordon thought he'd found the girl of his dreams. But women like Sarah are tough to hang on to.

When she causes the disappearance of a mob boss's priceless Chihuahua, she disappears herself, and the odds Gordon will see his lover again shrivel like nuts in a polar plunge.

With both money and love lost, he's going to have to kill some SOBs to get them back.